FROM THE
NANCY DREW FILES

THE CASE: Nancy tries to put the brakes on a case of criminal mischief that could lead to murder.

CONTACT: Nancy's friend George is number one on the bike breaker's hit list.

SUSPECTS: Erik Olson—For Erik, the bike trip has become an ego trip. Competition is his middle name, and he's decided that George is the one to beat.

Kendra Matthews—She joined the trip to get close to a guy . . . a guy who's shown a clear interest in getting close to George.

Michael Kirby—He shows up in a van, claiming to sell sporting goods, but Nancy suspects he's only trying to take George for a ride.

COMPLICATIONS: Her best friend is in danger, and Nancy has no idea why. If she slips up once, if her investigation takes one false turn, it's George who could end up paying.

D0829743

Books in The Nancy Drew Files® Series

#1 SECRETS CAN KILL
#2 DEADLY INTENT
#3 MURDER ON ICE
#4 SMILE AND SAY MURDER
#5 HIT AND RUN HOLIDAY
#6 WHITE WATER TERROR
#7 DEADLY DOUBLES
#8 TWO POINTS TO MURDER
#9 FALSE MOVES
#10 BURIED SECRETS
#11 HEART OF DANGER
#12 FATAL RANSOM
#13 WINGS OF FEAR
#14 THIS SIDE OF EVIL
#15 TRIAL BY FIRE
#16 NEVER SAY DIE
#17 STAY TUNED FOR DANGER
#18 CIRCLE OF EVIL
#19 SISTERS IN CRIME
#20 VERY DEADLY YOURS
#21 RECIPE FOR MURDER
#22 FATAL ATTRACTION
#23 SINISTER PARADISE
#24 TILL DEATH DO US PART
#25 RICH AND DANGEROUS
#26 PLAYING WITH FIRE
#27 MOST LIKELY TO DIE
#28 THE BLACK WIDOW
#29 PURE POISON
#30 DEATH BY DESIGN
#31 TROUBLE IN TAHITI
#32 HIGH MARKS FOR MALICE
#33 DANGER IN DISGUISE
#34 VANISHING ACT
#35 BAD MEDICINE
#36 OVER THE EDGE
#37 LAST DANCE
#38 THE FINAL SCENE
#39 THE SUSPECT NEXT DOOR
#40 SHADOW OF A DOUBT
#41 SOMETHING TO HIDE
#42 THE WRONG CHEMISTRY
#43 FALSE IMPRESSIONS

#44 SCENT OF DANGER
#45 OUT OF BOUNDS
#46 WIN, PLACE OR DIE
#47 FLIRTING WITH DANGER
#48 A DATE WITH DECEPTION
#49 PORTRAIT IN CRIME
#50 DEEP SECRETS
#51 A MODEL CRIME
#52 DANGER FOR HIRE
#53 TRAIL OF LIES
#54 COLD AS ICE
#55 DON'T LOOK TWICE
#56 MAKE NO MISTAKE
#57 INTO THIN AIR
#58 HOT PURSUIT
#59 HIGH RISK
#60 POISON PEN
#61 SWEET REVENGE
#62 EASY MARKS
#63 MIXED SIGNALS
#64 THE WRONG TRACK
#65 FINAL NOTES
#66 TALL, DARK AND DEADLY
#67 NOBODY'S BUSINESS
#68 CROSSCURRENTS
#69 RUNNING SCARED
#70 CUTTING EDGE
#71 HOT TRACKS
#72 SWISS SECRETS
#73 RENDEZVOUS IN ROME
#74 GREEK ODYSSEY
#75 A TALENT FOR MURDER
#76 THE PERFECT PLOT
#77 DANGER ON PARADE
#78 UPDATE ON CRIME
#79 NO LAUGHING MATTER
#80 POWER OF SUGGESTION
#81 MAKING WAVES
#82 DANGEROUS RELATIONS
#83 DIAMOND DECEIT
#84 CHOOSING SIDES
#85 SEA OF SUSPICION
#86 LET'S TALK TERROR
#87 MOVING TARGET

Available from ARCHWAY Paperbacks

The Nancy Drew Files™

Case 87

Moving Target

Carolyn Keene

AN ARCHWAY PAPERBACK
Published by POCKET BOOKS
New York   London   Toronto   Sydney   Tokyo   Singapore

AN ARCHWAY PAPERBACK *Original*

 An Archway Paperback published by
POCKET BOOKS, a division of Simon & Schuster Inc.
1230 Avenue of the Americas, New York, NY 10020

Copyright © 1993 Simon & Schuster Inc.
Produced by Mega-Books of New York, Inc.

ISBN: 0-671-79479-5

First Archway Paperback printing September 1993

10 9 8 7 6 5 4 3 2 1

NANCY DREW, AN ARCHWAY PAPERBACK and colophon are registered trademarks of Simon & Schuster Inc.

THE NANCY DREW FILES is a trademark of Simon & Schuster Inc.

Cover art by Tricia Zimic

Printed in the U.S.A.

IL 6+

Moving Target

Chapter

One

NOT FOR ME!" Nancy Drew held up her hand to halt Ned Nickerson, who was about to put another helping of pasta on her plate. "One more mouthful," she continued, her blue eyes sparkling mischievously, "and you'll have to roll me out of here."

"Can't have that," Ned replied, grinning. He looked across the table at Nancy's friend, George Fayne. "George?"

The dark-haired girl shook her head and groaned. "I think I've reached my limit, too," she replied. "But ask the waiter if we can take the rest with us," she added. "It'll be a great carbo-load in the morning before we start off."

"Spaghetti for breakfast?" The disdain in Kendra Matthews's voice was unmistakable, and she wrinkled her nose disapprovingly.

1

"Not to worry," said George cheerfully, deliberately ignoring the put-down as she peered into the large crockery bowl on the table. "I don't think there's enough for both of us." She glanced over at Nancy. "Too bad Bess isn't here," she said. "She would have *loved* this dinner!" She paused. "Of course, she would have had to start a new diet tomorrow, too!"

"You're probably right," Nancy agreed. Bess Marvin, George's cousin, was usually along when Nancy and George went anywhere, but sports were not her strong suit, so she had decided to pass on the bike trip.

Ned, a student at Emerson College, had invited Nancy and George to join a group of students for a three-day bike trip during Emerson's fall weekend. The spaghetti dinner at a small, family-style Italian restaurant just off campus had been planned so the cyclists could meet one another before the ride.

Besides Kendra Matthews, the girls had met CJ Springer, a tall, blond biology major whose studious appearance behind rimless glasses contrasted sharply with his muscular build. And then there was Erik Olson, who was leading the group and who had taken every opportunity during dinner to remind the rest of the group that he was Emerson's top cyclist.

"You'll need all the help you can get if you want to keep up with me," Erik said to George.

She had told him that she was competing in the women's division of the same thirty-kilometer race he had signed up for the following month.

"I just finished a ride in Colorado," he continued, before she had a chance to respond. "Uphill, high altitude. Not much oxygen up there. That's where you separate the pros from the amateurs. You *have* to be physically fit."

"I thought this was a recreational ride, not a race," said Nancy, attempting to head off a clash between George and Erik.

"Every ride is a race," Erik said. "And I've never been in better shape." A slight smile that was more like a sneer crossed his face. He turned to George. "But unless I'm mistaken, you walked in here tonight favoring your left leg."

Even in the muted candlelight of the restaurant Nancy could see George's face flush. "I twisted my knee last week," she said defensively. "But it'll be totally healed by next month."

"We'll see," said Erik.

"Well, you two can race all you like," said Kendra. "I signed up for this bike trip so I could get better acquainted with one CJ Springer." She slipped her small, beautifully manicured hand over CJ's big one and smiled up at him.

Nancy noticed that several expensive rings flashed on her fingers. They went right along with the designer sports outfit she wore. Obviously Kendra Matthews was not hurting for money.

CJ cleared his throat, and Nancy could sense his embarrassment. He seemed to be a shy person, not used to this kind of open attention.

"I think a man with brawn and brains is a real prize," Kendra cooed, seemingly unaware of CJ's discomfort.

Despite her dislike for Kendra's boldness and insensitive approach, Nancy had to admit that her own motives weren't so different from Kendra's. She had signed up for the trip so she and Ned would have some time together. With her busy schedule and Ned in classes, they hadn't been able to spend much time together lately.

"It's too bad the other girl who's going couldn't be here tonight," Nancy said. "What's her name? Jennifer?"

Erik nodded. "Jennifer Bover. She works nights at Ed's Diner, on the other side of town. I don't think anybody really knows her." He looked around at the other Emerson students, and there was a general shaking of heads. "All I know is that she's a transfer student and she's in my psych class. She just signed up for the trip yesterday."

"Well, we'll meet Jennifer tomorrow," said Ned, getting up. "Tonight we should probably get some sleep."

Once outside, they gathered on the sidewalk in front of the restaurant to recheck last minute details.

"Rats!" said George. "I forgot my breakfast."

"I'll get it," Nancy said quickly. Even though George claimed that her knee had almost completely healed, Nancy was concerned about her friend walking any more than necessary. She darted back into the restaurant and returned a few moments later, carrying the carton of spaghetti.

"See you all in the morning," Erik said. "I'm going to jog around campus once before I hit the dorm." He looked over at George. "Would you care to join me?" he asked.

"Negative," said George, scowling after him as he jogged off without waiting for an answer. "There goes Mr. Personality!" George said. "I wonder if they cover behavior modification in that psych class he's taking."

CJ, who was standing next to George, grinned. "Take care of that knee," he said quietly, leaning over so she could hear him. "Ice it tonight and sleep with it propped up. It might help."

George smiled back at him. "Thanks," she said. "I will."

Kendra tapped her foot on the sidewalk, openly annoyed with the attention CJ was paying George. She reached for his arm and tossed her long black hair back over her shoulder with an impatient gesture. "I think it's time to go," she said to CJ.

"Right!" He turned to the trio beside him. "Would you guys like a lift? I'm in the parking lot over there."

Nancy looked at George, once again thinking about her knee.

"No, thanks," George replied quickly. "We're going to walk back across campus. See you tomorrow."

Nancy, George, and Ned crossed the street, heading toward Packard Hall, the Emerson dorm in which George and Nancy had been given a room.

"You could have taken a ride," Nancy said to George.

George grinned. "If I'd accepted a ride, I might never have reached the dorm alive," she quipped. "Talk about territorial rights. Kendra's got him staked out and barb-wired."

Ned laughed. "That's what it looks like, but it's definitely a one-sided attraction. CJ and I have a couple of classes together, and we've gotten friendly."

"I liked him," George said, in her usual forthright way. "But the two of them together seem like the world's biggest mismatch."

"You've got that right," Ned replied. "Kendra's been pursuing him since the semester began. She even signed up for molecular biology just because he was in the class. That's how she heard he was going on the bike trip. He'll shake loose, but he's a nice guy, and he'll do it his way. He certainly doesn't encourage her." Ned slipped his arm around Nancy's shoulders.

The night was clear, and the air was crisp with

the smell of autumn. Overhead, thousands of stars shimmered against the midnight blue sky. It was a perfect fall night in the Midwest, and it promised a perfect long weekend for nature lovers and cyclists.

"What's that building over there?" George asked, pointing toward a large brick structure with a dome on top.

"That's the science observatory," Ned answered, "and the one coming up here on our left is the president's house. That's the back of it we're seeing. It faces the road over there, but the back is as pretty as the front."

"I heard on TV that Emerson's president has gone to France," Nancy said. "Something about an award? I'm trying to remember."

"Your memory's doing fine," said Ned. "He and his wife were invited to accept an award for Emerson's student exchange program. It's one of the best in the nation. They left yesterday."

The trio was parallel to the spacious back gardens of the three-story house, where the lawns sloped down to a deck and swimming pool, covered now for the off-season. Beyond the pool, Nancy could see a small, low, glassed-in building adjoining the back of the mansion. It looked like a hothouse.

As often happened with them, Ned was reading her thoughts. "The president used to teach botany," he explained. "He just couldn't give it up when he got into administration. I understand that he grows all sorts of exotic plants in there— even orchids." Ned gestured toward the darkened rear of the house, but Nancy was already staring in that direction.

"Ned, I saw a light over there. Someone's out on the patio." She squinted for a better look and pointed. "See? By the French doors. He's wearing a ski mask! It's got to be a burglar."

With that, Nancy bolted across the lawn, up toward the building. But the intruder must have seen her coming, for he moved quickly around the far side of the house, out of view. Nancy ran full speed around the mansion. Ned, surprised by Nancy's quick reaction, hesitated a moment, then broke into a run behind her, with George following.

The masked person, dressed in dark pants and a dark turtleneck, was racing toward a motorcycle parked in the driveway.

Nancy could feel her heart pounding as she ran across the front lawn. She was gaining on him. Only thirty feet separated them now.

As agile and quick as a panther, the prowler jumped on the motorcycle and started it up.

Nancy ran out into the driveway, still determined to catch him. But instead of heading for the street, he suddenly whirled the bike around and, revving the engine, aimed the motorcycle directly at her!

Chapter

Two

NANCY LEAPT to the grass, barely getting out of the way in time. Furious, she raised her arm and hurled the carton of spaghetti, hitting the man on the motorcycle squarely on the side of his head. He lost his balance and almost tipped over. As Ned and George came into view, the motorcyclist regained his balance, made a U-turn in the driveway, and sped off, disappearing down the street.

"Are you all right?" Ned asked, breathing hard as he ran to Nancy's side. "He aimed that bike right for you!"

"I know," Nancy said grimly. "I clobbered the side of his head, but it didn't stop him."

"What did you throw?" George asked, coming up behind them.

Nancy turned to her friend. "You don't want to know," she said, attempting to lighten a scary situation.

"That's what I thought," said George. "My breakfast."

"Let's get to a phone," Nancy said. "I've got to call the police. He was carrying a backpack, and my guess is that it's filled with stuff from the president's house."

"Packard Hall is the closest dorm. We can cut across here," Ned said, pointing. "There's a phone in the lobby."

Nancy ran on ahead and within minutes had alerted the Emersonville police to the burglary. By the time George and Ned reached the building, the alarm had gone out to cars in the area.

"I'll bet it's the same guy who pulled the other robberies around town," Ned told them as they sat in the lounge, which, typically for a dorm on a Friday night, was almost deserted. "He's really clever. He pulls just one robbery a week—although come to think of it, if it's the same guy, he pulled two robberies this week, one on Monday or Tuesday night that didn't get reported until"—he hesitated—"Wednesday, I think, when the people came home. The guy only hits in the rich areas of town, and always when the owners are away. The papers are full of it. People are buying alarm systems like they're pizzas. He only takes jewels or cash, and none of the jewels have shown up in local pawnshops. The police think he's working with an out-of-town fence."

"The officer I talked to said they had two cars in the area. He thought they might have a chance of getting him this time," Nancy said. "He said the other burglaries weren't even discovered until the following day."

The phone in the lobby rang, and the student who answered it peered into the lounge.

"Call for Nancy Drew," she said.

The call was brief. When Nancy came back into the large room, it was apparent from her expression that the news was good.

"They've got him!" she said. "One of the cars picked him up two blocks from campus." She gave Ned and George a wide grin. "He was easy to recognize. He was the only motorcycle rider in the area who was wearing cold spaghetti."

"Way to go, Nan!" George said, laughing.

Ned laughed, too.

Nancy turned to Ned. "I have to go down to headquarters," she said.

"I'll drive you," he offered. "My car's close. I'll cut through the back way to the parking lot and meet you out in front."

"Thanks," Nancy said. "I'll get George some ice for her knee and meet you in a few minutes."

George had sprawled out on one of the couches in the room and had her leg propped up. "You're okay, Nancy Drew," she said with mock seriousness. "I'm not sure I could walk from here to the kitchen. It was that after-dinner run that did it!"

Nancy grinned at her and returned in a few minutes with a towel filled with ice cubes. "Some insurance for tomorrow's ride," she said, handing it to George.

"Thanks," said George. "I'll wait here till you get back." She motioned toward the TV set near the couch. "Maybe I'll catch the sports roundup. Besides, I want to hear all the details—especially about my spaghetti."

When Nancy and Ned reached the police station, they waited a long time in Lieutenant Easterling's office, while the president's sister identified some of the jewelry that had been taken. Finally Nancy was called in to give her statement.

Lieutenant Easterling was a big man with a soft voice and a kind face. Nancy had worked with him before, and he greeted her like an old friend.

"Are you going to be in town over the weekend, Nancy?" he asked her when she had finished giving her statement.

"No, I'm going on a bike trip. I won't be back till late Monday," Nancy explained.

"Well, we probably won't need you again," he said, although his voice sounded uncertain.

"When I get back to the dorm, I can call you and let you know our itinerary," she added just in case. "You can reach me by phone when we stop for the night."

"Fair enough," Lieutenant Easterling said. "And, Nancy, thanks. This was a big break for our department. I'm glad you were around."

Nancy and Ned walked back out to his car. It was late, the evening was gone, and they'd hardly had a chance to say two words to each other.

"How about a cup of coffee and a piece of pie?" Ned asked as they got into the car.

"Coffee sounds great," said Nancy. "Pie sounds impossible on top of that dinner."

"Not for me," said Ned, putting the key into the ignition. "I've heard that Ed's Diner makes the best pie in town. Let's go. Maybe we'll have a chance to meet Jennifer Bover before tomorrow."

Nancy looked at her watch. "Depending on when her shift ends, we could even give her a lift back to the dorm. Kendra said Jennifer was living in Packard."

Ned drove through the quiet, darkened streets away from the campus toward the highway. "I hear that Ed's Diner is popular with truckers," he said, as they left the residential area. "A lot of them swing off the freeway so they can eat there."

"Then the food must be good," Nancy said.

Once they were on the highway, it was only a short drive to the diner. Nancy pointed up ahead at a flashing neon sign. "There it is."

Ned pulled into a parking space in front of Ed's Diner, and the couple went inside. The place was bigger than it appeared from the outside, and business was brisk, even at that late hour. The worn padded booths, taped in places to hide the cracks in the vinyl coverings, clearly announced that this was an eating place that had been around for a long time.

Nancy slipped into an empty booth near the cash register, and Ned seated himself opposite her.

"I wonder which one is Jennifer," Nancy said, looking around at the three waitresses who were hustling to fill orders.

The cashier, who was also doing hostess duties, finally appeared at their table with two coffee mugs in one hand and a steaming pot of coffee in the other.

"Sorry you had to wait," she said. "We're shorthanded tonight, and the place has been cracklin' like a house afire! Coffee?" She was a short woman, about twenty pounds overweight, and had sparkling gray eyes that were surrounded by permanent laugh wrinkles. She looked like somebody's grandmother.

Nancy nodded. "Please," she said.

"I want some pie, too," Ned said. "Do you have apple?"

"Sure do. Best apple pie in town."

"With ice cream," Ned added. "And can you

14

tell us which one of the waitresses is Jennifer Bover?"

The woman's friendly expression suddenly disappeared. "Jennifer Bover?" she repeated, her voice taking on a sarcastic ring. "Miss Jennifer decided to call in sick twenty minutes before her shift started. She knew that Helen was on vacation. And she knew that the night manager was off. And she knows what Friday night is like around here. But does she care about the rest of us? No! Then on top of it, yesterday, she asked for the weekend off to go on some kind of biking trip."

She glanced from Nancy to Ned, who were both looking puzzled at the outburst, and forced a small smile. "I'm sorry," she apologized. "I shouldn't mouth off like that. Are you friends of Jennifer's?" She paused for a split second and then answered her own question. "No, you can't be friends, or you wouldn't have asked which waitress she was. . . . I'll get your pie."

"What do you think of all that?" Ned asked Nancy when the woman was out of earshot. "If Jennifer's sick tonight, I wonder if she'll be going on the bike trip."

Nancy shrugged. "Guess we'll have to wait till tomorrow and see if she shows up," she replied. "Right now, I'm worrying about something more important."

"What's that?"

15

"Are you going to let me have a bite of your pie?"

Ned laughed. "Only if you're very, very good."

When they got back to campus, Nancy and Ned sat in silence in front of Packard Hall, just enjoying being together. Nancy nestled contentedly against his shoulder as he held her in his arms.

"I love you, Nancy Drew," he whispered into the soft reddish gold waves that cascaded to her shoulders. "And I've missed you. I can't believe we're going to have three quiet days together."

"Isn't it wonderful?" Nancy murmured. She pulled back a little and looked up into his brown eyes. She cupped his face between her hands and gently kissed him. "Oh, Ned—" she said, but her sentence went unfinished as he returned her kiss. When he finally released her, she leaned back against the soft leather seat cushions and sighed. "I'd better go in or I'll never get up in the morning. It must be almost midnight."

Ned looked at his watch. "Almost," he said, getting out. "You're right, I should get back to the frat house, too." He walked to Nancy's side of the car and opened the door, and the two of them walked slowly arm in arm to the door of Packard Hall.

"Tomorrow," Ned said. He planted a quick kiss on Nancy's forehead and strode back to the car as she entered the dorm.

The lobby was quiet, and Nancy paused to glance into the dimly lit lounge. A girl wearing jeans and a sweatshirt was standing across the room by a picture window, looking out across campus.

"George?" Nancy whispered, wondering why her friend was up and about.

The girl jumped at the sound of Nancy's voice and quickly turned around.

"I'm sorry," Nancy apologized. "I didn't mean to startle you. I thought you were someone else." She grinned. "But I see that my someone else is off in dreamland over there." She motioned toward a couch where George was curled up, asleep. "I'm Nancy Drew," she continued, extending her hand.

"Jennifer Bover," said the young woman, shaking hands. She pulled off the bandanna covering her head and ran her fingers through her short, golden blond hair. Nancy couldn't help staring. Except for her hair color, she did look a lot like George. "Nice to meet you, Nancy," she said with a smile.

"Well, I'm pleased to meet *you*," Nancy said. "I hear we're going on the same bike trip. I'm sorry you couldn't be at the dinner tonight— although you didn't miss anything except some good food. I'm really psyched for this trip, aren't you?"

"I'm anxious to get away for a few days," Jennifer replied. "But I'm not a very experienced

17

cyclist. They said that didn't matter when I signed up."

"I'm sure that's not important. It's just a fun trip, not a competition," Nancy said. "And the weather's going to be perfect."

Jennifer nodded and then yawned. "Excuse me, I'm exhausted," she said. "I need to get upstairs and get some sleep. We have an early start, and I pulled a long, hard shift tonight." She moved toward the door.

Nancy looked at her, puzzled. "Where?" she asked.

Jennifer glanced back over her shoulder, her eyes making contact with Nancy's for a brief second before she looked away. "At Ed's Diner, on the other side of town."

Chapter

Three

THAT'S WEIRD, Nancy said to herself, staring after Jennifer. Why would she lie? She pushed the question from her mind and walked to the couch where George was sleeping. "Come on, George. Time to go upstairs and get into a real bed."

George stretched and propped herself up on one elbow. "What time is it?" she mumbled, rubbing her eyes.

"After midnight," Nancy said. "And I just had the strangest conversation with Jennifer Bover."

"Rover?" asked George. She yawned and swung her legs off the couch.

"Not Rover, Bover."

"Y'know, that couch is pretty comfortable."

Nancy grinned. "A bed will be even better." She knew from past experience that there was no point in trying to pursue a conversation with George when she was half asleep. "Let's go upstairs."

In the morning Nancy and George checked to make sure they had packed everything they'd need for the bike trip before they went down to join the others at breakfast.

"How's the knee?" Nancy asked.

"Feels fine," George replied. "I think the ice pack did it, but I'm taking my trusty knee support along just in case." She tucked the elasticized brace into the top of her small backpack. "There! I'm ready, I think. You know, I vaguely remember you saying something last night about a dog. Rover?" She paused. "Or was I dreaming?"

Nancy shook her head and laughed. "You weren't dreaming. But it was Bover, not Rover. A person, not a dog. Jennifer Bover, the one who's going on the bike trip."

"Oh, yeah," George said. "The one who couldn't have dinner with us because she had to work."

"Yes, except she wasn't working," Nancy said. Quickly she recapped the events of the evening for George. "The cashier at Ed's Diner told Ned and me that she had called in sick. Then half an hour later, I met her downstairs in the lounge and she told me she had pulled a long, hard shift. I can't figure out why she'd lie about it."

"Maybe she had a hot date," George said. "Or just wanted a night off."

"That would explain why she called in sick," Nancy said, "but why would she tell *me* she was working? It doesn't make any difference to me whether she was or not."

George shrugged. "Who knows?" She slapped Nancy on the back good-naturedly. "Wherever you go, you attract mysteries, Nan. They hide in the bushes just waiting. And when you pass by, they jump out and pinch your ankles and say, 'Here I am, here I am. Solve me. Solve me, Nancy Drew!' And you feel duty-bound to perform."

Nancy laughed as all five feet, eight inches of George crouched down beside the bed and pretended to jump out of the bushes and pinch at her ankles.

"You've already nailed a burglary suspect on this trip," George continued, "so now you can take a day off. Take three days off! This is going to be a relaxing weekend for both of us."

"You're right," said Nancy. "And you're a space case too, Fayne. But that's part of your charm."

George zipped up the top compartment of her backpack and slung it over her shoulder. Then she picked up her pannier, which contained most of her clothes and other gear. It looked like a saddle bag and would be attached to the back rack of her bicycle. "Let's go find something to eat."

The cyclists had agreed to meet in Packard Hall lounge, since three of the group—Nancy, George, and Jennifer—were staying there.

Jennifer was in the dining room when Nancy and George entered, and she waved at them to join her at a small table by the window.

"Sorry if I seemed rude last night," Jennifer said as Nancy and George brought their trays to her table. "Friday nights are always the busiest, and I was really zonked."

"Ned and I stopped at Ed's Diner last night for coffee," Nancy said slowly. She was curious why Jennifer would keep on with the lie but was hesitant about accusing her. After all, as George had said, it wasn't any of their business. "You must have gotten off before we got there."

Jennifer's gaze dropped to the table. "Yes, I left a little early," she said quickly. "I had a terrible migraine headache."

"Do you work every night?" Nancy asked, ignoring the kick to the ankle that George gave her under the table.

Jennifer seemed to be relieved to have the subject changed. "No, just four nights a week. I have some night classes this semester."

"Erik told us that you're a transfer student. Do you like Emerson?"

"I love it," Jennifer said. "I transferred here from a community college in upstate New York because Emerson has one of the best early childhood education programs in the country. That's my major." She laughed. "It's a natural for me. I'm the oldest of six kids." She reached into a pocket of her backpack, which was on the floor next to her chair, and pulled out a wallet. She opened it and showed them a photograph. "Here —these are my brothers and sisters. My mom took this the day I left for Emerson."

Nancy looked at the informal shot and smiled. "They look like a lot of fun."

"They're pretty lively," said Jennifer.

"Boy, from a community college to a private school," George said. "You're talking big bucks on tuition."

Jennifer nodded. "It's pretty steep. That's why I'm working. I have a partial scholarship. My family could never afford it without that. This is my first experience away from home, but everybody's really friendly."

Ned and CJ were waiting in the lounge when the girls finished breakfast, and Nancy hurried over and gave Ned a hug while CJ went to talk to George and Jennifer.

"Anything more from Lieutenant Easterling?" he asked. "Are we cleared for flight?"

"We're cleared," she assured him. "I called him late last night and gave him our itinerary."

"Who's the blond talking to George?" he asked.

"That's Jennifer Bover," Nancy replied. "You know, the strangest thing happened last night after I got back here." She quickly told him about her conversation with Jennifer. "And then at breakfast, when I told her that we'd gone to Ed's Diner last night, she said she'd left early because of a migraine headache."

Ned's reaction was similar to George's. "I thought you promised me you weren't going to work on this trip," he teased. "But anything with a hint of a mystery hooks you. Come on, Drew. Relax! We have three stressless days ahead."

"Got it," she said, smiling at him. But whatever else she was going to say was cut off as Erik bounded in, carrying several boxes. He exuded self-confidence that bordered on arrogance. It was apparent that he considered himself the leader of the group.

"Are we ready?" he asked in a loud voice. He held up the boxes. "I just picked up our lunches from the cafeteria."

George, who was anxious to get on the road, got up from the couch where she had been sitting with Jennifer and CJ.

"Glad to see you can stand on that leg this morning," he said, "or was that story about a bad knee just a handy excuse to be used in case of failure?"

"Stuff it, Erik!" George snapped.

"Your hair looks great," he said to Jennifer, ignoring George. Jennifer acknowledged the compliment with a smile, and Erik turned his attention to Nancy.

"And why didn't you tell us last night," he

continued, "that you are *the* Nancy Drew, private investigator? You were mentioned on every radio newscast I heard while I was out doing laps this morning. You're quite the heroine!"

Kendra, the last one to arrive, briefly interrupted his monologue as she dragged her gear into the lounge.

Grateful for the diversion, Nancy smiled at her and raised her hand in greeting as Kendra sat down between Jennifer and CJ. But the gesture froze in midair as Nancy's eyes caught the look on Jennifer's face. The blond girl, who had been so friendly earlier, was now staring at her with a strange expression.

"So give us the inside scoop, Nancy Private-Eye," Erik said sarcastically. "What about this dangerous criminal you caught?"

"I'd rather not talk about it," Nancy said quietly, trying to keep her annoyance from showing. "Formal charges hadn't been filed when I left headquarters. Besides, Erik, I'm on vacation."

CJ looked over at Ned and motioned toward the door. "Time to hit the road," he said. He picked up his gear and headed outside.

"Stressless three days, my foot," Nancy whispered to Ned, as they followed the group. "I might *commit* a crime instead of solving one if Erik doesn't cool it!"

Ned grinned at her. "Once we get going he'll calm down," he assured her.

But when they got to the bike compound, it got worse instead of better. Nancy had just finished clipping the pannier she had borrowed from George to the rack on the back of her bike when she heard Erik talking to George.

"By the way," he said to her, "I talked to the sports reporter on the *Emerson Eagle*—that's the school paper. I tipped him off that you'd be on this ride and it would be sort of a dry run for the race next month."

"You *what?*" George spit out the words. "What are you talking about? You know that men and women don't compete against each other."

Erik shrugged his shoulders. "Of course I know that. But that's not to say that you and I can't compete this weekend. After all, you *are* a competitive cyclist. I told the reporter we'd be competing, but unofficially—and that I'd keep him posted on our times."

George glared at him but said nothing.

"Since this is a recreational ride," Erik continued, as he put on his helmet, "we'll compete in segments each day. We'll start timing when we hit the county road, and whoever comes up with the best total time over the three days wins. Agreed?"

"What choice do I have?" George snapped as she adjusted the strap of her helmet. "If I don't, I get labeled a poor sport."

But Erik didn't hear what she said. He had

already kicked up his stand and pushed off, leaving George sputtering.

It was a twenty-minute ride out of town to the little-used county road they were taking, and George and Erik rode neck and neck.

Overhead, the sun gently warmed them from an almost cloudless sky. Nancy pulled off her sweatshirt jacket and tied it around her waist. Her long-sleeved cotton shirt was ample covering for the autumn morning. The air was fresh and clean, and the softly rolling hills on the left were carpeted in green. To the right, stubble from a freshly harvested crop left neat rows in the brown soil, like a giant comb. It was a perfect day to be outdoors, away from phones, studies, work. Nancy looked over at Ned and grinned.

"This sure beats riding in a stuffy old car," she said. "Maybe we all need to go back to pedal power."

"It's great until it rains," he replied. "Or snows. Or until you have to pick up five visiting relatives at the airport."

At the first scheduled stop along the route, a fruit stand, Nancy took George aside while Ned and the others selected some apples and pears for their lunches.

"How's the knee?"

"It's fine. No problem at all this morning."

"You're doing great," Nancy said. "That was a dirty trick Erik pulled, telling the school paper you were competing, even unofficially, on this ride."

"I know," said George, "but I'll make it work to my advantage. It'll help me get in shape for the women's race next month."

"It's not going to help," came a voice from behind them.

George turned around quickly. Erik was standing behind them, smirking. "Didn't anyone ever teach you that it's not polite to eavesdrop?" she said.

But her sharp retort didn't faze him.

"I get some of my best information from eavesdropping," he said. "And you won't have to worry about the race next month. I don't think you'll be competing in it." His voice took on a false-solicitous tone as he continued. "Knees that have been damaged have a way of giving out unexpectedly. I predict that you'll be headed for the infirmary before this *recreational* run is over!"

Chapter

Four

GEORGE'S DARK EYES flashed with anger. "I have no intention of spending time in the infirmary," she snapped at Erik. "And I have every intention of winning this race."

"We'll see," Erik replied. He turned and walked over to his bike. "Let's go, everybody," he yelled at the rest of the group.

"He—he's insufferable!" George sputtered, swinging up onto her bike.

Nancy watched as George pedaled furiously to catch up with Erik. Then she turned to Ned, who had walked up beside her and overheard Erik's remark. "I'm worried about George," Nancy said. "That thing Erik said sounded like a threat to me. You don't think he'd do anything to hurt her, do you?"

Ned shook his head. "Erik is famous for his

bad attitude," he said. "It's just something you learn to ignore if you're around him much. And what could he do to hurt her? He can't lie about who wins with five witnesses riding along behind."

"I guess you're right," Nancy said, but she wasn't convinced.

Erik and George had ridden about a quarter mile ahead of the other cyclists on the first segment of the route, and they were pulling ahead again. Kendra was sticking close to CJ, who, although an experienced cyclist, was riding at a leisurely pace. Every so often Nancy would notice the small dark-haired girl engage him in conversation, and once, when she stopped to check a tire, she asked for his help, which he willingly gave.

Jennifer, riding behind Kendra and CJ, had been noticeably quiet. Nancy pulled up alongside her.

"You said you're from New York State, right? I hear there are some great bike trails there," Nancy said.

"Some," Jennifer replied. Her eyes met Nancy's briefly. Then she pedaled harder and pulled away from the group, avoiding further conversation.

When they reached a picnic area around noon, they were all ready for a rest and some food. The roadside stop was rustic and somewhat neglected, with tall grass growing up around the legs of the wooden tables and benches, and deep ruts in the gravel parking area in front. Tall pine trees ringed the picnic site, and in a nearby clearing was a weathered seesaw and swing set.

"Bike racks are on the other side of the rest rooms," Erik yelled as the five slower cyclists pulled into the gravel parking lot. "Lock 'em up!"

George, who had been carrying one of the lunch boxes in her pannier, had already claimed a picnic table and was laying out the food that the Emerson cafeteria had prepared for them. The picnic area was deserted, except for their group and a family with two little boys. The children were playing on the seesaw.

"This seat taken?" CJ asked George, as he lifted one long leg over the bench. He sat down beside her without waiting for an answer and reached for a ham and cheese sandwich. Kendra raised an eyebrow and sat down on the other side of the table beside Nancy and Ned.

CJ pushed his blond hair back from his forehead and grinned at George. "You're giving him a good run for his money," CJ said quietly, nodding toward Erik, who was leaning up against a tree talking to Jennifer. "But you were favoring that left leg again when you were setting out lunch."

George nodded. "It's aching again. I'll wrap it before we leave here."

"CJ, pass me an apple," Kendra said, reaching across the table to tug on his shirt sleeve.

Her ploy to divert CJ's attention from George was so obvious that Nancy had to bite the insides of her cheeks to keep from grinning.

They were planning their next stop of the afternoon when a blue minivan that Nancy had seen on the road earlier pulled into the parking area by the rest rooms. A door slammed, and a few minutes later a handsome, dark-haired man with the husky good looks of an athlete walked confidently over to the table.

Nancy guessed his age at about twenty-five.

"Michael Kirby," he said to Ned, who was at the far end of the table. He thrust out his hand. "Mind if I join you?" he asked, after Ned had made introductions. "I hate to eat alone."

"Sit down," Ned replied, and everyone on the bench shifted to make room. "You're one of the few people we've seen since we left town. This road is really off the beaten track."

Michael pulled out a sandwich and a bag of chips and started to eat. "Yeah, not much traffic out here, except for farm equipment. I saw you at that fruit stand before I turned off for Kenville. I thought I might run into you here."

"Do you live around here, Michael?" Kendra asked, flashing him an engaging smile.

"No. But I cover this territory regularly. I sell athletic equipment. I hit all the little towns off the beaten path." He passed his bag of chips to Kendra. "Actually," he continued, "my company's thinking about sponsoring a cyclist in the big race next month. I thought I'd sort of check out your group and size up the two leaders. See if I could pick us a winner."

"What company do you represent?" CJ asked, looking over at Michael's van, which was unmarked.

"American Sportstyle, and a couple of others," Michael said, following CJ's gaze. "And if you're wondering why the van doesn't have a company name, it's because I've been robbed one time too many."

"I *was* wondering," CJ said.

"Well, I'll tell you. You put a name on the van and everybody knows you could be hauling expensive sports equipment—bikes, accessories, weight benches. My van's been broken into so many times that the advertising wasn't worth it."

"Out here?" George asked.

"Out here," he repeated. "Not everybody you meet on this route is a clean-cut athlete or part of a picnicking family." He nodded his head toward the children, who were riding on the ancient swings with Jennifer pushing them. "I can vouch for that." He took another few bites of his sandwich, then waggled a finger at George. "That's a nice bike you've got," he said. "Noticed it when you pulled into the fruit stand. You were flying! New?"

"Yes," George said. "As a matter of fact, it is. And I love it. This is the first time I've had it out on a long ride."

"Do you live in Emerson?" he asked.

"No," she said.

"Student?"

George nodded absently and reached for a cookie.

"Bike like you've got costs plenty," Michael said, munching on the last of his chips.

When George didn't volunteer any information, Michael laughed. "I guess what the papers say must be true. College kids have more money to spend than any other age group in the country." He licked his fingers and stood up. "Well, I've got to be getting on my way. I may run into you again later, down the road. I have to make a couple of stops in town, around here." He turned to Ned. "Are you staying at Bannon House tonight?"

Ned nodded. "Bannon House tonight and then Lakeview tomorrow. Then we circle around through Woodside and back to Emerson by Monday night."

"Good route! County fair is on in Bannon," Michael said. He flashed a smile at Kendra. "Great rock group on the program—Timeline. Maybe I'll see you there." He walked to the rest rooms, and a few minutes later the van pulled out of the parking area.

"Okay, everybody," Erik said, walking over to the table. "Social time is over. Let's go!"

"Just a minute," George said. She had unzipped her backpack and was rummaging through the contents. "That's weird," she muttered to herself. "I know I put it in here."

"What are you looking for?" Nancy asked.

"My knee support. Nan, I'm losing it! I *know* I put that thing in here this morning. I'm sure I didn't put it in my pannier."

Nancy frowned. "I saw you put it on top in your backpack, then zip it up."

"Well, it's not here now."

CJ, who was watching the search, heaved his backpack up to the bench and unzipped it. "Not to worry," he said. "I always carry one. You can use mine. Here"—he rapped his knuckles on the bench—"sit down and put your leg up here. I'll help you." He took an elasticized knee brace from his pack while George sat down.

"Well, what is this?" Kendra asked, walking toward the couple. She stared at CJ. "The resident doctor, are you?" she asked sarcastically.

"A biology major is as close as you're going to get to a medic on this trip," he replied without looking up.

"There, that should do it," he said to George, giving the brace a final pat. "Too tight?"

"No, it feels good," she said. "Thanks."

"Any time." He took her hand as she swung her leg off the bench and stood up.

Kendra had moved over toward the grove of trees and was talking animatedly to Jennifer. The family with the children had left, and Erik, who'd been watching off to one side, walked over to

George and CJ. "I see you're getting closer to the infirmary," he commented. Then he turned around. "Okay," he yelled. "Everybody over here!" He waited for Kendra and Jennifer to join the group before he continued. "Now, this next stretch of road is a little more challenging than the one this morning."

"He sounds like a tour guide," Nancy whispered to Jennifer, who nodded and moved away.

"It winds around, in and out of hollows, and you'll run into some uphill grades—nothing major if you've ridden in Colorado, but enough to give you a workout. Oh, and keep on the pavement as much as you can. There's loose gravel on the shoulders and a deep gully for drainage on our side of the road. Let's go!"

He swiveled around and marched off toward the bikes, flanked by Kendra and Jennifer.

"Something weird is going on here," Nancy said to Ned as they followed CJ and George to the bike racks. "I saw her put that brace in there this morning. I saw her zip the pack. Somebody has to have taken it."

"But who'd steal a knee brace?" Ned asked.

"Well, I can think of two people who don't have George at the top of their Best Friends list. Kendra's furious with her because CJ's paying too much attention to her, and Erik is so jealous of her being able to keep up with him that he'd do almost anything to keep George from winning."

She reached up with both hands and lifted her

hair off the back of her neck. "It's like he has a compulsion to win—at any cost."

Ned shrugged. "I don't know what we can do about it," he said. "Except keep an eye on George"—he grinned at Nancy—"which CJ seems to be doing a good job of." His voice became serious. "Nan, there's no proof that anyone stole the brace. Maybe she *did* forget it."

"Ned, she did *not* forget it. I saw her put it in her backpack." The exasperation in Nancy's voice was obvious. "Somebody in the group must have taken it."

"Or the guy who came for lunch," Ned said.

"No, it couldn't have been him," Nancy said. "He wasn't anywhere near her things. But while we're on the subject, I didn't like him very much."

"Why not?"

"Well, he was asking George all those questions—about where she lived and if she was a student and about her bike. I just didn't like him."

They unlocked their bikes, checked to make sure that the tires didn't need air, then followed the others out to the road.

Erik had been right about the route, Nancy thought, later that afternoon. There were sudden curves and dips in the road. In addition, the stately elms that lined the way had already dropped some of their leaves, and those, together with puddles from a recent rain, made parts of the road slick. There was little conversation among the riders. Everyone was too busy concentrating on safely maneuvering the route.

Nancy was keeping a close eye on Erik and George, who were not riding quite as far ahead of the group as they had been that morning. But to Nancy's dismay, Erik was definitely in the lead. She took a curve, shifted gears, and worked at pumping uphill. It was getting late in the afternoon, and she was thinking of how good a hot shower would feel, when suddenly George disappeared from view.

Nancy put on a burst of speed, racing ahead of the group. At the top of the hill she braked, skidded, and jumped off her bike, scanning the road in front of her. Then she noticed something off to the side and realized it was a person, not a thing.

It was George—and she was lying motionless in the deep gully.

Chapter
Five

"George!" NANCY YELLED, sliding down the slope to reach her friend. "George!"

Filled with concern, she crouched down beside the tall girl, who now lay so still in the mud and leaves of the gully. George groaned quietly and tried to move. Nancy reached for the water bottle on her friend's crippled bike, pulled the scarf from her neck and doused it with water. Very gently, she wiped George's forehead. The side of George's cheek was scraped from the brambles she'd slid over when she was thrown from her bike, but she didn't appear to have any major cuts.

Nancy just hoped that George didn't have any serious injuries. Slowly George's eyes opened. She blinked twice and moved one arm, then the other, as if testing to see that everything was working.

"Boy," George said weakly, "that was a surprise." She bent her left leg at the braced knee and then tried the right one. Both moved freely. "Just checking," she said to Nancy.

"Can you sit up?" Nancy asked, cradling her arm under George's shoulders. "Is your head all right? I mean, I've heard about people getting head injuries even when they're wearing a helmet."

George banged on the helmet with a fist. "As all right as it's ever been," she quipped, grinning at Nancy.

"You know what I mean," Nancy said, with just a trace of impatience in her voice. "It's not funny, George. You could have been seriously hurt."

"Actually, I landed on one shoulder, but it seems to be okay." She carefully moved her shoulders back and forth as Nancy helped her to sit. She looked up as Ned and CJ slid down the embankment. "Oh, good grief," she said. "I'm about to become Exhibit A. I hate to have everybody staring at me. I'm fine. Really!" She stood up, still somewhat wobbly, and brushed the leaves and mud from her clothes.

Nancy could tell that she was embarrassed by all the attention.

"I'm just a klutz, that's all," George muttered.

With CJ supporting her on one side and Nancy

on the other, they made their way back to the side of the road, while Ned carried the disabled bike up to the shoulder where the rest of the group was waiting. Erik, on hearing Nancy yell, had turned around and come back. As if that weren't bad enough, just then Michael Kirby happened to drive by, and Kendra and Jennifer flagged him down. He pulled his blue van over to the side of the road and got out.

"What happened, darlin'?" Michael asked George.

Nancy saw George wince. Anyone who knew George knew that calling her "darlin'" wouldn't go over well.

George shook her head. "I shifted gears, and the next thing I knew I was in the ditch. I don't know what happened." She paced off the area of the accident, examining the road surface. "There are no potholes here, no big rocks, no slippery spots. It doesn't make any sense."

"Well, don't look at me," said Erik, his tone belligerent. "I was a good eighth of a mile ahead of you when you did your swan dive. Probably your knee gave out," he continued, with a trace of smugness, "and you lost your balance."

"My knee was fine," George retorted, unconsciously moving her hands to the brace that firmly supported the knee. "No problem. I don't know what happened."

"I think I do," said Nancy. She was crouched down beside the bike with CJ, examining the

41

brakes. "Your brake cables popped." She paused. "And it looks as if it wasn't an accident."

"You're kidding!" said George. "But who—"

Michael moved away from the girls and squatted down beside Nancy to inspect the brakes. "This probably came defective from the factory," Michael said. "You can't believe the slipshod workmanship that goes into things these days. I mean, everybody knows about the recall rate on cars. Bikes are no better. Some guy on the line at the factory has a bad day and presto! Some unlucky customer gets a defective bike."

"Not a Cannondale," Nancy said. "It's one of the best bikes you can buy. Cannondale has an excellent reputation." She stared up at him. "Which I thought you'd know, since your line of work is sporting goods."

"Well, pardon me," said Michael.

"Besides," Nancy continued, ignoring his sarcasm, "these brakes have been tampered with. It looks like someone deliberately cut them just enough so that when George was going downhill and put on her brakes, the cables popped."

CJ, who was also down on his knees beside the bike, stood up and put his arm around George. "I have to agree with Nancy," he said to her, oblivious to the angry glare he was getting from Kendra. "Somebody messed with your bike, and you're lucky you weren't seriously injured."

"Well, whatever exciting little story you want

to cook up to tell your friends is okay with me," Michael said. He turned to George. "But meanwhile, darlin', it looks like you're without wheels. I'd be glad to give you a lift to the next town. I was on my way to the fair there when I passed by. We can load the bike in the back of the van."

George hesitated, glancing from CJ to Nancy. It was clear that she didn't want to ride with Michael Kirby.

"Well, are you coming or not?" Michael said. "I don't bite."

"Let's move it," said Erik impatiently. "You don't have many options, Fayne, unless you want to walk your bike to Bannon House. It's about five miles."

"Do you think you can ride a bike?" CJ asked George quietly, quickly sizing up the situation.

She nodded, her dark curls bobbing.

"Then take mine," CJ said to her. "I'll ride with Michael. We'll put your bike in the van and fix it when we get to the inn. I've got extra cable if you don't."

George looked up at him and grinned. "I always carry extra cable, and I've got my tools, but I could sure use the help. Thanks!"

"It's a smart thing to do, anyway," CJ said, "to get back on a bike. I was in an accident two years ago, and my coach borrowed a bike for me and made me get right back on and keep going. Getting thrown like that is a real shock." He picked up George's bike and walked to the van, where Michael was waiting. "Change of passengers," CJ said to Michael.

"Fine with me," Michael replied, slamming the driver's door.

Nancy's usually cheerful face was serious as she observed the group. First the missing knee brace, Nancy thought, and now this "accident." Who would want to hurt George? Erik was certainly a possibility. He really wanted to win this "recreational" run. It seemed hard to believe that he'd take their informal race so seriously, Nancy thought. But he had told the *Eagle* about their supposed contest, and it wouldn't look good if the paper printed that he had lost. And from what she had seen he was a total egomaniac.

Then there was Kendra, who was clearly jealous about CJ's attention to George. No, Nancy thought. She just couldn't imagine Kendra's knowing enough about a bike to cut the cables. Nancy couldn't even imagine the girl holding a pair of pliers! But it *would* be like Kendra to convince someone to help her.

Nancy turned and looked over at Jennifer, who was talking to Ned. Was Jennifer a possibility? She had seemed so friendly at first, but after Erik made a fuss about Nancy being a private investigator, she had pointedly distanced herself from Nancy and George. Was she just shy, or was she hiding something? But she had signed up for the trip at the last minute and didn't seem to know much more about bikes than Kendra.

And when would anyone have had the opportunity to tamper with the bike? It would have to have been during their lunch break.

"I don't understand who would sabotage my bike," George said to Nancy as the van pulled out.

"Well, *you* might, George."

Nancy detected the distinctive scent of Kendra's expensive perfume and knew, before she turned around, who had spoken the barbed words.

"I mean, after all," Kendra continued, "staging an accident—just a teeny one where you're not really badly hurt—is a great way to get attention, isn't it?" Her eyes flashed with jealousy as she confronted George. "If it's attention you want, you may get more than you bargained for."

"What's that supposed to mean?" George asked. "Is that a threat?"

"No, only a warning." She flicked a piece of fluff from her hot pink track suit. "Then again, maybe you just need to get training wheels until you learn how to ride."

Ned, who had gone to check the brakes on the other bikes, came and stood by Nancy just in time to hear Kendra's final remark. "We need to get going," he said briskly. "We don't have much daylight left."

"Good idea," Erik agreed. "I've heard enough of your garbage, Kendra. Chill out."

George looked up quickly, surprised at this defense from an unexpected source. But her relief was short-lived as Erik continued. "It's hard enough riding with amateurs who don't look after their equipment"—he looked pointedly at George—"without having to listen to junk like that from people who have no reason to be here except to advance their social life."

"Just what do you mean by that crack?" Kendra asked.

"I mean," Erik said, "that some people don't know the difference between a bike trip and a dating service."

Kendra's pretty face twisted into an ugly mask as she faced Erik. "And some people," she snapped, "don't know the difference between a bike trip and an ego trip. Why don't you explain to us, Erik, why it is that every time you sign up for one of these outings, somebody has an accident?"

Erik flushed, and Nancy could see the cords in his neck straining, as his anger surfaced. But before he could say a word, Kendra stormed on. "Why don't you tell us the story about Jeffrey Long, Erik. Or maybe you'd like me to tell it. You almost *killed* him!"

Chapter

Six

ERIK TURNED his back on Kendra and moved toward his bike without answering. He kicked back the stand, swung his leg over the crossbar, and started out, pedaling fiercely. George, not about to give up on their competition, quickly followed, leaving the rest of the group standing by the side of the road.

Nancy grabbed Kendra's arm. "Tell me about Jeffrey Long," she demanded.

Angrily Kendra shook Nancy's hand away. "You're the detective. You figure it out!"

Less than an hour later, Nancy braked as the group approached the bike compound at Bannon House.

Built in the late nineteenth century, the prim two-story farmhouse had been given an addition- al wing later to accommodate a second generation of the Bannon family. When working the land no longer yielded sufficient income, one of the heirs had turned the place into a country inn. Its edge-of-town location and proximity to the main bike trails had made it a natural stopping place for cyclists.

As Nancy locked up her bike, she noticed that at least two dozen bicycles were already parked there. Obviously the Emerson group wasn't the only one taking advantage of the fall break.

When Nancy signed in at the desk in the main hall, she was told by the desk clerk that she would be in room twenty-two with George, who had signed in fifteen minutes earlier.

Nancy's anger at Kendra and Erik had not diminished during the five-mile ride. "I've got to find a phone," she said to Ned, as he signed in. "The Emerson police should be able to tell me about Jeffrey Long, whoever he is. If Kendra thinks I'm not going to check this out, she's in for a big surprise."

He smiled at her and nodded. "CJ and I are bunking together. I'll take your stuff up to your room while you make the call. And we'll keep an eye on George."

Nancy gave him a quick hug and a grateful look. "Thanks, Nickerson," she said, and then grinned. "I may keep you around." She turned to the woman at the desk. "Is there a pay phone around that I can use?" The woman pointed to the game room in the back.

The room was deserted except for two college-age guys shooting pool at the far end. Nancy assumed they were with one of the groups whose bicycles she had seen outside. The phones were against a wall, sandwiched between a dart board and a large relief map of the area. Nancy walked over, picked up the receiver, and dialed.

"Emersonville Police Headquarters, Sergeant O'Malley here," said a male voice.

"This is Nancy Drew. Is Lieutenant Easterling available?" She drummed her fingers on the counter beneath the wall phone while the sergeant checked. Then Lieutenant Easterling's familiar baritone voice came on the line.

"Nancy! How's the ride?"

"More exciting than I expected," she replied. "Can you do me a favor?"

"Sure."

"Will you see if you have anything about a bike accident in Emersonville involving a Jeffrey Long? I'm not sure when it happened." Nancy mentally computed a time frame. If Kendra was a junior now and had been on campus then . . . "It would have been within the last two years," she added.

"Okay. I'm going to put you on hold."

Lieutenant Easterling came back on a few minutes later, but the news was disappointing. "Nothing in our records," he said. "But you know, I vaguely remember that name. Long was an Emerson student, right? There was something in the newspaper. . . . Tell you what. Give me your number, and I'll get back to you in a few minutes. I'm going to call campus security."

"Great!" said Nancy. "While you're at it, ask them if they have anything on Erik Olson or Kendra Matthews, will you?"

"Sure," he replied. "What number are you at?"

Nancy squinted at the ancient phone and read off the number. "Will it take long?" she asked. "I'm at a pay phone in the game room."

"Shouldn't," Lieutenant Easterling said. "The campus records are computerized."

"Thanks!" She hung up and looked around the large room. Wood-paneled walls and a beamed ceiling fit in perfectly with the rustic setting. There was a Ping-Pong table parallel to the pool table, and couches with overstuffed cushions sat under a long window that offered views of the forest beyond. The other wall was dominated by a massive stone fireplace.

It was a perfect room for relaxing in after a day's ride, and she could tell why the inn was popular with cyclists. Nancy took a magazine from a wall rack and curled up on the couch to wait. It seemed like hours before the phone rang. She jumped up and grabbed the receiver.

"Well, you picked a couple of winners," Lieutenant Easterling said cheerfully. "Olson was involved in that accident with Jeffrey Long. Seems like they were both signed up for a race last year, but Long had an accident with his bike the week before and never got into the marathon."

"What kind of an accident?" Nancy asked.

"A freak accident. His wheel came off when he was on a training run. He broke an arm and some ribs, and one of his lungs was punctured. The kid was hurt really badly. He's recovered now. Olson had borrowed Long's bike the day before the accident. They were fraternity brothers. Olson was suspected of tampering, but nothing was ever proved. In fact, no charges were filed, which explains why we don't have a record of the incident."

"What about Kendra Matthews?" she asked.

"Matthews is another story," he said. "She's on campus probation this semester. In May she tore up the room of some gal who went out with her ex-boyfriend. And according to Mike—he's the campus cop I talked to—she's a spoiled brat. Too much money and mouth, and too little maturity and brains. Her father's some bigwig attorney."

"Thanks, Lieutenant," Nancy said. "Anything new on the burglaries?"

"Nope. Spaghetti Man isn't talking, and we haven't found any more of the stolen property. He's local. Works as night manager at Ed's Diner. Or did. Well, keep in touch."

"What?" Nancy said, but the dial tone was already humming in her ear. She replaced the receiver and leaned up against the wall. Ed's Diner! That had to be more than coincidence. And it might explain why Jennifer was so stand-offish after she heard about Nancy's involvement in the capture. If Jennifer and the burglar both worked at the diner, they must know each other. Nancy walked quickly out of the game room.

"Erik Olson," she said crisply to the woman at the desk. "What room is he in?"

"Twenty-nine."

"Thanks." Nancy turned and quickly walked up the stairs to the second floor.

She paused in front of the door to room twenty-nine and took a deep breath. Then she raised her hand and banged on the door with her fist.

The look of surprise on Erik's face when he opened the door was unmistakable. "Well, well. I, uh, didn't expect to see you," he stammered.

"I'll bet you didn't," Nancy said, pushing past him into the small room.

"Hey, what do you think you're doing?"

"I'm inviting myself in," said Nancy, "unless you'd like to step outside and discuss this in front of anyone who happens to come by."

"Discuss what?" Erik asked warily.

"Jeffrey Long's 'accident,' for starters. It seems you have an unlucky habit of being around people who ride bikes that fall apart. The Emerson campus police had some questions about that being an accident."

"Wait a minute!" Erik said angrily. "They didn't prove anything. A couple of guys in the frat house who were on my case set me up for that." He stared at her with gray-blue eyes that were as cold as icicles. "Didn't they tell you that the case was closed for lack of evidence?"

"They did," Nancy said. "But they weren't convinced you were innocent, either." She was looking past Erik when she replied, gazing across the room at the hook on his closet door. "But we don't lack evidence here, do we?"

Erik's eyes followed her glance. He moved toward the closet, but Nancy was quicker. She snatched an object hanging from the hook and whirled around to face him, holding George's knee support in her hand.

"Wait a minute," Erik said as a red flush crept up his neck. "That was just a joke. Can't you take a joke? Are you always so serious?"

"You bet I'm serious when my best friend is at risk!" Nancy snapped. "I don't see anything funny about this. And I don't see any humor in sabotaging her bicycle, either. She could have broken her neck."

"Hold on," Erik protested. "So I stole her stupid knee brace, but I didn't touch her bike." He held up his hand as if taking an oath. "I swear it. On my honor."

Nancy gave him a withering look. "Right. I'm warning you, Erik," she said in a low voice. "If you have any more tricks up your sleeve to harm

George or to keep her from finishing this ride, you're going to have to answer to me."

She stormed out and hurried down the hall to the room she was sharing with George.

"Nancy!"

Ned's voice stopped her just before she reached the door. He was coming up the stairs two at a time, grinning at her. "I've been sent to find you," he said, giving her a hug. "George and CJ are in the compound working on her bike. Come on down and tell us what's happening."

"Oh, Ned," she said, as they went downstairs. "That Erik is such a . . . sleazeball!"

George and CJ stopped working while Nancy told them Lieutenant Easterling's information on Erik and Kendra, and described her confrontation with Erik.

"Do you think he did it?" George asked, pushing her hair back as she gripped a pair of pliers.

"I don't know," Nancy said. "He stole your knee brace for sure." She tossed it to George. "But he was adamant about the bike. He says he didn't touch it."

"I vaguely remember hearing about Long," Ned said.

"I was on an exchange program in Europe," said CJ. He made no comment on the information about Kendra.

"One other thing," Nancy said. "The burglar

they arrested last night is the night manager at Ed's Diner."

George looked at her, startled. "Then Jennifer must know him."

Nancy nodded. "But I don't know where that fits in with everything else yet. Anyway, how's the repair job going?"

"Slow," George said. "But it could have been a lot worse. None of the spokes are broken, and nothing else is bent or damaged."

"Where's the rest of the group?" Nancy asked.

"Jennifer's in her room. She's not hungry. Believe it or not, Kendra went with Michael Kirby to the rock concert at the fair," Ned said, raising his eyebrows. "And there goes Erik with that group that came in just before us."

"Well, I'm starving," Nancy said. "There has to be food at the fairgrounds. How far is it, do you know?"

"Less than a mile," Ned replied. "We can leave the bikes here and walk."

"You two go on ahead," George said. "We'll finish up and meet you at the grandstand."

Nancy and Ned had no trouble finding the fairgrounds. Everyone was heading in that direction and the hurdy-gurdy music of the midway rolled out on the evening breeze, as did the smells of the animal barns that housed the livestock. They got some chili burgers and fries from one of the booths, then found seats in the grandstand behind Michael and Kendra just as the concert started. George and CJ finally arrived at the intermission.

"Mission completed?" Ned asked.

"All fixed and ready to ride," said CJ. "I've even given it a trial run. That bike is as safe as a baby carriage."

"As safe but not as slow, right?" George asked.

"Right!" said CJ, smiling at her affectionately. He handed her a hot dog and a can of soda from the cardboard tray he was carrying. "Here, this will take the edge off your appetite."

Kendra, who had pointedly ignored the arrival of CJ and George, turned to Michael.

"I've heard enough of this hick band," she said. "Let's go."

They disappeared into the crowd, and the foursome settled in on the bleachers for the second half of the concert.

"You know what I want to do?" Nancy said to Ned, after a couple of numbers.

"What am I now?" he asked her. "A swami? A crystal-ball reader?"

"Come on, Ned! What do I always want to do at a fair?"

Ned groaned. "I hoped we could avoid it this time," he said. "You want to ride the Ferris wheel, right?"

"Right!" Nancy said brightly. She turned to CJ

and George. "We're going to the midway. We'll meet you back here when the concert's over."

Hand in hand, Ned and Nancy strolled away from the concert area and over toward the midway. There was a large crowd in front of the Ferris wheel.

"Popular ride," Ned said. "The line seems awfully long to me."

"That's because everybody loves the Ferris wheel," Nancy teased. "Except maybe one or two misfits."

"Excuse me, madam," Ned said as the line began moving. "Are you insulting me?"

Nancy started to answer, but then touched her finger to her lips. Familiar voices were drifting over from the other side of a popcorn stand.

"She staged that accident just to get CJ to pay attention to her," Kendra wailed. "She knew he was my property for this trip."

"Not to worry, sweetheart," Michael Kirby replied. "I have a feeling that"—he laughed—"George isn't going to finish this bike trip, anyway!"

Chapter

Seven

NANCY GRASPED Ned's arm tightly, and a worried expression crossed her face. "Ned! That was a threat if I ever heard one."

"Now, don't jump to conclusions, Nancy," Ned said. "He may have been talking about the trouble George has had with her knee."

"Ned, I have a funny feeling about him," Nancy said. "I'm going back to warn George. I'm not going to let her out of my sight for a minute." She stepped out of the line and headed for the bleachers, with Ned following.

"Do me a favor?" she asked over her shoulder. "Keep CJ busy while I talk to George. And I want to take a look at Michael's van. No point in getting everybody upset about this."

Ned nodded. The concert was just ending, and streams of people were leaving the stands. Nancy spotted the tall couple coming toward them and waved. "Come on," she said, running over to George and linking arms with her. "I want to show you something." She hurried George toward the building that housed the crafts, homemade jams, and baked goods. "We'll be back in a little while," she shouted at Ned and CJ.

"What's up?" George asked, puzzled by Nancy's urgency. "Could you kidnap me later, Nan? I was kind of enjoying the company of a tall blond."

"Sorry, George," Nancy said as they entered the building, "but this kidnapping was necessary." A long table displaying handmade afghans and quilts was just inside the door. Nancy paused by the table. "George," she said, "when you first saw Michael and CJ at Bannon House with your bike, what did Michael say to you?"

George shrugged. "He just said he'd be glad to give me a lift back to Kenville."

"Just you. Not you and CJ."

George nodded.

"That's the second time he's offered to take you somewhere, right? The first time at the side of the road, and again at the Bannon compound."

"Yes. What are you getting at, Nan?"

"It's as if he's trying to separate you from the group," Nancy said. "I don't like it."

George grinned. "Are you discounting my feminine appeal, Ms. Drew?" She posed like a model, with one hand behind her head. "He probably just can't resist my newest scent, Eau du Cycle. Boy, was I glad to get into a shower!"

Despite her concern, Nancy grinned. "George, I think CJ will vouch for your appeal, but I'm concerned about Michael Kirby. He's spending a lot of time with our group—almost as if he's following us—but he doesn't know any of us. For a salesman, he doesn't seem to be selling anything, and for a sporting goods rep, he didn't think about the liability factor when your bike broke down. Something about him doesn't ring true.

"And," Nancy added, taking a deep breath, "Ned and I just heard him tell Kendra that you weren't going to finish this bike trip!"

George's breath caught in her throat, and she looked at Nancy in surprise. "What?" she asked.

"He said you weren't going to finish the ride," Nancy repeated. "It sounded like a threat to me."

George frowned. "What now?" she asked in a shaky voice.

"I want to check out his van," Nancy said, "while he and Kendra are at the midway. I figure we've got time if we can find it in the lot."

"CJ and I passed it on the way in. I know where it's parked," George said. "Let's go out the back way, it's closer."

The two girls weaved through the jammed parking lot until they spotted the blue van.

"Keep an eye out for them," Nancy said,

digging in her purse. "I think I can pop open that back door."

"You don't have to," George whispered. She had just tried the door on the passenger side. "Kendra didn't lock her side."

"All the better."

Quickly Nancy got in, then opened the glove compartment and examined the contents, while George stood watch. No registration papers. Sunglasses. Flashlight. Maps. She lifted out the maps. "Look at this!" she said.

George turned and looked inside. Nancy was pointing to a revolver.

"Standard equipment for a salesman," George quipped. But the quaver in her voice told Nancy she was frightened.

Nancy probed under the seat and pulled out a file folder. "This is weird," she said. She thumbed through the newspaper clippings in the folder. "These are all about the recent burglaries in Emersonville. Including one about last night's arrest." She reached over for a briefcase on the backseat.

"Nan, move it! They're coming!"

Instantly Nancy jumped out of the van, pushed the door closed, and followed George. Crouching behind a pickup truck two rows over, they watched as Michael and Kendra climbed into the van and drove off.

"Too bad you didn't have time to get into the briefcase," George said.

"I know," Nancy said. "But I did notice something. The initials KS were stamped on the case. I'm wondering if Michael Kirby is really Michael Kirby."

"Interesting," said George. "And I took a quick look in the back. No salesman's sample cases in sight. No catalogs. Who is this guy?"

Nancy shook her head. "I don't know, but I intend to find out."

Nancy and George wandered back through the midway until they spotted Ned and CJ at a ring-toss booth. Ned was carrying a panda bear, and CJ had a stuffed elephant under one arm.

"Looks as if you two did all right," Nancy said as she stood on tiptoe and gave Ned a kiss on the cheek.

"And how did you do?" he whispered in her ear, handing her the panda.

"Fair," she whispered back. "I want to find a phone." She held the panda up in front of her and continued in a normal tone. "Thanks! He's a great-looking guy. Does he have a name?"

Ned grinned. "Not yet. You can christen him later. Right now, if we don't get CJ to some food, we'll have to carry him back, and I'm not up for that."

Nancy looked over at CJ and nodded. "It'd take all three of us to move that hunk," she teased. "It'll be easier to feed him."

"And me!" said George. "I'm so hungry I

could eat"—she hugged the stuffed toy that CJ had given her—"I could eat an elephant!"

"There's a restaurant down the road," Ned said. "Let's try that."

With arms linked, the two couples strolled out of the fairgrounds, heading toward one of the two lighted buildings on the main street.

The restaurant was noisy and jammed with people. Nancy looked around quickly. There was no sign of Michael and Kendra, but Erik was sitting with a group at a large table. She recognized two of the group as the guys who had been playing pool in the game room earlier.

"They must be with the cycling club from up north," CJ said.

"Yes, the desk clerk told me that three groups are staying at Bannon House this weekend," Ned replied. "Ours is the smallest." He waved at a couple sitting at the back of the restaurant. "I played football against that guy last fall," he explained.

Nancy scanned the room for a table. "Unfortunately, it looks as if that's the only vacancy," she said, pointing at an empty table beside Erik's group.

"That's all right," said George. "We don't have to socialize. All I want to do is E-A-T!"

Erik looked up as they approached, and a genial smile crossed his face. "Hey, park yourselves," he said, waving at them. He nodded at the student sitting at the end of the table. "Pull that table over," he ordered him, waving his hand. "The more the merrier. I'll do the introductions."

The student jumped up and pulled the empty table next to theirs as Erik called out names.

"What's put him in such a good mood?" George muttered.

"Not me," Nancy whispered back at her. "Last time I talked to him he could have cheerfully killed me."

"Erik has been telling us about his rigorous training program for you guys," one of the women at the table said. "You're really lucky to have him leading your group."

"Just can't believe our good fortune," George mumbled to Nancy, as she sat down.

CJ leaned over her shoulder. "Keep cool," he said. "Ned and I will go place the orders. What'll you have?"

"Cheeseburger, fries, and a ginger ale," said George.

"Got it," replied CJ, grinning. He and Ned walked to the counter to place their orders, and Nancy turned to the student beside her.

"My friend George here," she said, nodding her head at the dark-haired girl, "will be in the thirty-kilometer race next month. Are any of you competing?"

"Are you kidding?" asked the young woman. "That's for serious bikers like Erik. I'm surprised that your friend even signed up for it. From what Erik has been telling us, she——"

George glared across the table at Erik. "She what, Erik? What have you been telling them? Why don't you tell *me*?"

Erik smirked. "Your knee is probably going to keep you out of this race," he said. "From what I saw today, you're about as agile as——" He looked across the table at the stuffed toy in her arms. George was already getting up. "As an elephant!" he shouted after her as she ran out of the restaurant.

Nancy caught up with George outside. "I'm sorry, George," she said, putting her arms around her. "Don't pay any attention to that jerk."

"It's not just Erik," George said, sniffing. "It's *everything!* My knee brace disappears, my bike is sabotaged. Then this weird nonsalesman who carries a gun shows up and keeps offering me rides, and Kendra and Jennifer are both giving me the deep freeze. And Erik insults me publicly. I should never have come on this bike trip."

"But then I wouldn't have met you," CJ said, coming up to the two girls.

"True," George replied, managing a weak grin. "Did we get any food?"

"Nope. I killed the order when I saw you leave. Do you want to go back in?"

"Not if I were dying," George said. She motioned to a store across the street. "The general store is still open. They should have some munchies."

"What happened in there?" CJ asked.

George started to explain to CJ as Ned arrived and Nancy took his hand. "We'll meet you in front of the store," she said to them. She quickly told Ned what they had found in Michael's van, as she led him across the street to a phone booth. "This shouldn't take long," she said, and handed him the panda. Ned leaned up against the booth to wait.

When she came out, she looked glum. Ned handed her the panda, and she hugged it as she said, "The only Michael Kirby the police have a record on is fifty-three years old and serving time."

The two of them headed down the street to meet up with George and CJ. The store, the only other lighted building on Main Street, also served as a bus station, according to a sign outside. CJ and George were sitting on the rickety steps outside, munching on cheese and crackers. "Want some dinner?" George offered, extending the cracker box.

"Actually," said Nancy, climbing the steps, "I have my heart set on an ice cream bar."

"Dessert!" said George. "Sounds good."

The four of them trooped inside and headed toward the freezer.

"Don't you kids ever go home?" asked the man

behind the counter. "I'm about ready to lock up. Where are you from, anyway?"

"We're on a bike trip from Emerson College," Ned answered. "We won't be long. We just want some ice cream bars."

"Emerson, huh? Well, I had one of your bunch in here tonight earlier, asking about a post office and a bus to Cleveland."

Nancy frowned. "What did this person look like?" she asked.

"Didn't notice," the man replied grumpily.

"But can you remember anything about the person? Anything at all," Nancy persisted.

He scowled. "She had kinda blond hair and was 'bout that tall." He wagged a finger at George, then shook his head.

"For the life of me," he said, "I can't figure why she was so desperate to get out of town."

Chapter

Eight

"SOUNDS LIKE JENNIFER," Ned whispered to Nancy.

She nodded slightly as the man continued. He seemed to be warming up to his subject now.

"She was wearin' kind of a bright green sweat-shirt. I remember the shirt because I said she must be Irish. Said she wasn't. Didn't talk much. She didn't exactly ask for Cleveland. Said she wanted a bus that didn't go to Emersonville. I told her that no more buses were coming through tonight, but a bus headed for Cleveland would be coming through on Monday. She seemed real disappointed. And then she left without buying anything but a newspaper."

"Thanks for your help," Nancy told him, letting Ned pay for the ice cream bars. When they were outside again, she turned to him. "Why would Jennifer want to catch a bus? A bus that did *not* go to Emerson?"

Ned shrugged. "I haven't the foggiest idea."

"Asking about a post office is odd, too," George said. "What would she have to mail?"

CJ looked from one to the other and shook his head. "Boy, you guys are something else," he said good-naturedly. "You can make a mystery out of almost anything. She didn't go to the fair, so she stayed in her room and wrote a letter to her boyfriend or her mother or something!"

"Maybe you're right," George said. She was feeling guilty that they hadn't told CJ about Michael's threat or finding the gun in his van, and he didn't know that Jennifer had lied about working on Friday night. Nancy had asked George to keep it quiet because until they had more information, talking about it would only cast more suspicion on people who might be innocent.

"You up for a game of Ping-Pong?" Ned asked Nancy as they approached Bannon House. Lights were still burning in the game room, although most of the rooms upstairs were dark.

"Not tonight," Nancy said. "George and I have some stuff we have to take care of." She ignored George's surprised look and continued. "But I bet CJ will take you on. We'll see you guys in the morning." Her panda under one arm, she grabbed George's arm with her free hand and hurried her off toward the stairs.

"Boy," said George as they walked down the second-floor hallway toward their room. "You sure can wreck a girl's love life pretty fast. You don't even let me get walked to the door." She tipped her head to one side as though deep in thought. "Let's see," she said slowly. "This 'stuff' we have to take care of. It wouldn't have anything to do with Jennifer, would it?"

Nancy laughed. "As a matter of fact, yes." She pointed to a sliver of light showing under the door of the room almost directly across from theirs. "Look, somebody's up."

"She's rooming with the charming Ms. Matthews, right?"

Nancy nodded. She knocked gently on the door. There was no answer. She knocked again.

"Strange," said George. "Maybe she's gone somewhere."

"Only one way to find out," said Nancy. She put her hand on the knob and turned it slowly. The door was unlocked. Gently she pushed it open and stepped into the room, with George behind her. The small light on the dressing table between the two beds cast a dim light in the room. A cluster of pill bottles and cosmetics covered one side of the table, next to an empty bed. The other side held only an alarm clock.

Jennifer was sleeping in the second bed, the blanket drawn up to her chin.

"We'll talk to her in the morning," Nancy whispered, motioning for George to back out.

Suddenly Jennifer sat up, startled, grabbed a book, and flung it at them. George held up the stuffed animal to deflect the book.

"Jennifer, it's okay. It's Nancy and George." Nancy reached over and quickly flicked on the overhead light.

"Okay?" Jennifer's voice wavered. "You scared the life out of me! What are you doing in here?"

"Look, we're sorry we frightened you, but we saw the light on," said George. She picked up the book from where it lay in front of her and handed it back to Jennifer.

Jennifer's voice trembled. "Seeing a light on doesn't mean you can barge into someone's room."

"I know. We're sorry," Nancy said quickly. "We shouldn't have come in, but the door was unlocked."

"The door was unlocked because Kendra came back from the fair to get something, and she left her key on the bed when she went out again." Jennifer pulled her knees up and tucked the blanket around her legs. "What do you want her for?"

Nancy moved closer to the bed. "Actually, I

71

wanted to talk to you. I was curious about why you asked at the store about a bus—"

"And why you were looking for a post office," George chimed in.

"What?" Jennifer said. "Since when is it a crime to ask about a post office? Or a bus schedule?"

"I thought you might be planning to check out on us," Nancy replied. "A lot of strange things have happened in the last twenty-four hours, including George's 'accident.'"

"I didn't have anything to do with that!" Jennifer's eyes darted from one to the other, and an undertone of fear crept into her voice. "You believe me, don't you?" She looked away. "It's none of your business, but the truth is I'm not having much fun on this trip. I was thinking of cutting it short."

"But the store owner said you wanted a bus that *wasn't* going back to Emersonville," George said.

Jennifer shrugged. "Where else would I go? He must have misunderstood. And as for the post office, I have a monthly tuition plan, and the payment is overdue. Now are you satisfied? You can believe it or not."

"I'd like to believe it," Nancy said. "I really would."

For a minute she considered asking Jennifer why she'd lied about working at the diner the night before, and whether she knew the night manager who'd been arrested for the burglary. But then she reconsidered. Jennifer didn't seem ready to open up just yet.

George, who was standing silently by the bed, looked down at a newspaper thrown on the blanket. It was folded to the article about the burglary on the Emerson campus. Jennifer's eyes followed George's gaze and traveled back up to her face.

"Please leave," she said in a low voice.

"Just one more thing," said Nancy, turning as she reached the door. "Where's Kendra?"

Jennifer shook her head. "I have no idea. Somewhere with Michael."

"See you tomorrow," Nancy said, and opened the door.

"Whew!" whispered George, once they were out in the hall and the door to Jennifer's room was closed. "That's one nervous lady. Do you believe the story about the tuition payment?"

"No," Nancy said. "I think she's scared and lying. But why? That's what I can't figure out."

"Did you notice what she'd been reading in the paper?" George went on.

Nancy nodded. "The article about the Emerson burglary. Everybody seems to be interested in that crime. First Michael, with his file of clippings. Now Jennifer. I noticed you looking at the nightstand. What was all that stuff?"

"Three prescription bottles with Kendra's name on them. One was something for allergies. I couldn't read the labels on the others. The rest of it was cosmetics."

"Do you have your key?" Nancy asked, as they walked across the hall to the room they were sharing.

George nodded. "Here," she said, thrusting the stuffed elephant at Nancy. "Hold Charley."

"Charley?"

"Charles Jonathan, actually. I named him after CJ," she explained, as she took the key out of her pocket. "You know, Nan, he's really a special person." She slipped the key into the lock. "I'll be glad to crawl into bed tonight. I'm exhausted." She pushed open the door and flicked on the light. "Nan!"

Quickly Nancy moved past her and entered. The room was in shambles. Things were strewn on the floor and on the beds. Everything in their panniers had been dumped. Nancy's backpack had been emptied and discarded in a corner, and the pocket on George's had been ripped out.

Nancy bent over and picked up a brown paper bag on the floor by the door. Scrawled on it in heavy black ink were the words: Get off my turf!

Chapter
Nine

"THAT HAS TO BE intended for me," George muttered as she looked over Nancy's shoulder at the note. "And I'll bet my bike on the identity of the writer." She pushed her mutilated pack aside and sat down on the bed, hugging Charley around the middle.

Nancy turned to face her. "George," she said slowly. "Maybe you need to call it quits. Drop out of the bike trip. Bess could come and pick you up."

George forced a lopsided smile. "This is not exactly a friendly greeting," she said, waving her arm at the mess. "But, Nan, we know Kendra has both skills and experience in messing up rooms, and I'm not going to cave in to *her!* I promise I'll be careful, but I'm not going back early."

"Okay." Nancy sighed. She had known before

she suggested it that George wouldn't leave early. "I'm going down to the registration desk. I'll be back in a few minutes."

"Nan, it's almost midnight. Nobody's going to be there."

Nancy grinned at George and set her panda bear down beside her. "That's what I'm counting on," she said. "Take care of brother bear." She was out the door before George could answer.

Nancy quickly ran down the stairs and glanced around. Night lights were burning in the lobby. No one was in sight.

Nancy tiptoed to the desk and fumbled in her fanny pack for the small flashlight she carried on her key chain. The guest register was still open on the counter. Smoothing out the paper-bag note, she compared the writing on it to the signatures in the book. It only took a minute to confirm her suspicions. She clicked off the flashlight and hurried quietly back upstairs to room twenty-two.

George had picked up some of their things and was sitting on the bed, surrounded by her biking gear. She looked up as Nancy came in.

"What's up?" she asked.

Nancy smiled wryly. "I just ran a handwriting check on our bag here. Kendra did it. No question about it. The handwriting matches her signature in the guest register. Big swooping *O*'s and backhand slant. She wrote the note, but I'm not convinced she trashed our things."

"Come on, Nan," said George. Her voice sounded tired. "She's got a history of this sort of thing."

"I know. I'll talk to her tomorrow. Thanks for straightening up. Between us, we can pick up the rest in no time. Then let's get some sleep."

"Best idea I've heard in the past hour," George said.

The next morning was gray and chilly, and Nancy topped her jeans with a V-neck sweater over a turtleneck shirt. "I guess summer is really over," she said to George, who was having trouble getting her eyes open.

"Can't you wait till morning to get up?" she mumbled at Nancy, squinting out of one eye.

"It *is* morning, silly," Nancy said. "Get up! You'll feel better when you get moving."

"Is that guaranteed?" George asked, stretching. Before Nancy could answer, she continued. "You look as if you're going somewhere. What's on the agenda? Besides biking, that is?"

"I'm going to have a talk with Kendra," Nancy said. She had the door open a crack and was looking across the hall. "But I'm waiting for Jennifer to leave their room. . . . And there she goes! Save me some breakfast," she said.

"Breakfast," George repeated. "Food. Food! I knew there was some good reason I should be out of bed." She jumped up and started dressing. Nancy chuckled and closed the door behind her.

Kendra was barely awake when Nancy knocked. She opened the door a crack and squinted at her. "What do you want?" she asked. She looked pale without her makeup, and there were dark rings under her eyes.

"I need to talk to you," Nancy said.

"About what?" Kendra asked belligerently, blocking the door. "I'm not even dressed."

"About this," Nancy said, pulling the paper-bag note out of her pocket.

"A grocery bag?" Kendra said. "You're kidding." She tried to shut the door, but Nancy's foot prevented it.

"No, I'm very serious," said Nancy. "If you prefer, we can talk about it at the breakfast table, and everyone else can join in."

Three guys from one of the other cycling groups came out of the room next door and gave a friendly wave to the girls. Nancy acknowledged the greeting and Kendra scowled. "Oh, come in," she said to Nancy. "I'd rather not stand out here in the hall looking like a refugee."

Nancy bit back a smile at Kendra's reference to her appearance, and reentered the room she had been in just the night before. Jennifer's bed was made, and her backpack was propped against the wall with her helmet beside it. Kendra's side of the room was a mess.

"Now, what is it you want, Ms. Detective?" Kendra snapped.

Nancy handed her the paper bag.

"'Get off my turf.'" Kendra read the words without feeling. "So why are you bringing this to me?"

"Because you wrote it," Nancy said.

"I did no such thing!" Kendra shrieked. She balled up the paper and threw it on the floor.

"Kendra," said Nancy, "last night while we were in town, someone vandalized our room—I mean really ransacked it—and left this note."

"So why come to me?" Kendra asked. "There must be fifty people staying at Bannon House."

"For two reasons," Nancy said. "First, you have a history of trashing people's rooms, especially when you get jealous. That's why you're on probation at Emerson."

Kendra flushed and lifted her chin defiantly. "That's a lie!" she said. "Do you believe everything you hear?"

"I believe what I hear from campus security," Nancy replied. "And we all know that you're steaming about George and CJ. Plus your handwriting matches the writing on the note."

"Well, I don't care what you say. I didn't write the stupid note, and I didn't trash your stupid room!" Kendra's voice kept rising as she went on. "I wasn't even here last night. I was out with Michael until after midnight. Ask Jennifer!"

"Seems as if you're getting pretty tight with Michael Kirby," Nancy prodded.

"What's it to you?" Kendra exploded. "Now get out of here!"

"I'm leaving," Nancy said. "But I'm warning you. If anything else happens to George Fayne on this trip, she's ready to press charges."

"We'll see about that!" Kendra snapped. "Do you know who my father is? Anthony P. Matthews the Third. That's right! Head of the biggest law firm in this county and a candidate for senate. You keep badgering me, and he'll have your head on a plate. Now you get out of here!"

Nancy started to go, but just before she crossed the threshold she turned back. "Just remember what I said."

Kendra slammed the door.

Nancy went downstairs and stepped out on the porch that ringed the big house on three sides. The air was crisp and cold, and the sun was breaking through the gloom, turning the dew on the leaves into sparkling crystals. What a beginning for the day! Nancy thought, as she went back inside to the dining room. The quiet, relaxing bike tour was not living up to its promise.

After a quick breakfast, Nancy excused herself to go to the game room to call the Emersonville police.

"I can't believe you're in the office on Sunday," she said, when Lieutenant Easterling answered.

"Not officially. I'm cleaning up some paperwork," he said. "What can I do for you, Nancy?"

"I wondered if you had recovered any of the stolen property from the other burglaries yet."

"Nope. And Palumbo—that's Spaghetti Man's name, Stephen Palumbo—he's not talking."

"What were some of the things stolen in the other break-ins?"

Nancy heard some papers rustling on the other end of the phone and imagined that the lieutenant was looking through a file. "Diamond rings, a fourteen-carat gold bracelet, an antique watch. The flashiest things on this list are the emeralds. Very old, very good, set in eighteen-carat gold, valued at fifty thousand. There was a necklace, earrings, and a bracelet. All square-cut stones."

"And Palumbo hasn't talked about a fence?"

"Nope. Can't get him to say a word. He came to Emerson a few months ago from Florida. Served time there for petty theft."

"Run me a couple of checks?"

"Sure. Name them."

"First, Jennifer Bover. She's an Emerson student who works part-time at Ed's Diner. She's on the bike tour with us."

"Ed's Diner? Now, that's a coincidence, isn't it? Bet she was surprised to hear that one of her co-workers got picked up Friday night."

"She hasn't said anything about it," Nancy said.

"Well, it was in all the newspapers," he replied.

Nancy thought about the paper on Jennifer's bed, folded to the article about the arrest.

"Second?" Lieutenant Easterling asked.

"Remember the check on Michael Kirby?"

"Yeah. We came up with the guy in Tennessee."

"Right. Can you contact the Florida police and find out Palumbo's connections there? Also, would you check out Michael Kirby with the Florida police, too? This could be an alias, though. His initials might be K. S. He's a Caucasian male, five-foot-ten, about one hundred and eighty pounds, muscular, curly black hair, twenty-five or so."

"We'll give it a whirl. I'll phone down south and talk to someone who worked on the Palumbo case in Florida. The computer won't spit out much on initials alone, though."

"I appreciate whatever you can do, Lieutenant. Oh, and will you check out his vehicle, too?" She gave him a description and the license number of Kirby's van. It was an Illinois license plate. "I'll check in with you later today."

"Okay. If I'm not here I'll leave the information with the desk sergeant. . . . Wait, hang on a minute, Nancy. Here's the readout on Bover. . . . There's nothing. A clean sheet. Do you want me to call the campus police about her?"

"No, thanks, anyway. I don't think they'll have anything. She just started a few weeks ago."

"Take care, Nancy," he cautioned.

"I will. Thanks for your help."

She hung up the receiver and walked to the bike compound. George had their things stacked on a picnic table just outside the compound, awaiting the group's departure. All seven water bottles were lined up on one end of the table, and Kendra was filling them from a pitcher of water. She pointedly ignored Nancy as she approached, turning her back to say something to Erik.

Nancy walked over to Ned, who was just inside the compound, putting air in one tire. "I can't believe I was freezing this morning!" she said as she peeled off her sweater and tied it around her waist.

"It's warming up," Ned agreed. "Indian summer. I just hope this lap is uneventful."

Nancy nodded. "Did George bring you up to date on what happened last night?"

He nodded toward the far side of the compound, where CJ was carefully inspecting George's bike.

"I'm not going to let that girl out of my sight," Nancy said.

"I think CJ's taken over in that department," he commented.

"Then we'll all watch her," said Nancy, following Ned into the enclosed area.

"Are you ready?" Erik called to George. He consulted a note pad as he walked over to where George and CJ were standing. "So far," he said smugly, "I have a three-minute-and-thirteen-second lead, and that will improve on this lap. It's uphill most of the way, and with my Colorado training I'll leave you in the dust."

"We'll see about that," said George.

All morning the riders struggled on the hilly terrain. Erik and George were ahead of the rest, with Erik leading.

The road wound through woodland, where the golds and russets of autumn turned the landscape into a patchwork of color. Here and there, a creek would meander out to the side of the road, only to disappear again into the woods. Once, from the crest of a hill, Nancy saw farm buildings off in the distance, with rectangular sections of plowed ground stretching out on the other side, but that was the only indication of human habitation.

The extra exertion demanded by the hilly terrain kept casual conversation to a minimum, and the lunch stop came as a welcome break.

A historic marker, set in concrete, stood guard in front of a picnic area, little used now that the main highway bypassed it. The brass plate announced that it had been a major stopping point on a pioneer trail as early settlers moved west. A stream trickled past the site, and the occasional screeching of jays in the woods beyond broke the calm silence.

Three pine picnic tables were lined up in a half-moon clearing, and a rusted metal can was upended in the center, covering a water pipe and faucet. The cyclists dismounted, and while the others started unpacking the food that the inn had supplied, CJ stretched out on one of the picnic benches and put his baseball hat over his face. "Thanks, I'm not hungry," he muttered, when George offered him a sandwich. "I really thought I was in better shape."

"You do look kind of pale," Nancy told him.

"Light-headed, that's all," CJ replied. "And hot." He raised his head and took a swig from his water bottle. "I'm glad it's flatter country this afternoon. I couldn't go up one more hill."

The banter at lunch was low-key. At the table beside them, Nancy heard Kendra complaining to Jennifer about Michael standing her up.

"He was supposed to meet me here for lunch," she pouted.

Nancy leaned over to Ned. "I'm glad he didn't make it," she whispered.

After they had finished eating, everyone packed up and headed for their bikes. CJ, who had remained sitting, finally got to his feet.

"Are you okay?" Ned asked, peering at him.

CJ shook his head. He reached for the table to steady himself and suddenly doubled over, arms wrapped around his midriff.

Ned ran to him, but he was too late. CJ had collapsed.

Chapter
Ten

NANCY AND GEORGE, walking toward their bikes, turned to call to the two boys to hurry up. They saw CJ fall and hurried back to kneel beside him.

"Give me your water bottles," Ned said as he cradled CJ's head in one arm, "and something to put under his head."

Quickly both girls passed over their bottles, and Nancy took her sweater from around her waist and rolled it into a pillow to go under CJ's head.

"What happened?" George asked Ned, as he held a water bottle up to CJ's lips. CJ did not respond, and the water dribbled to the ground.

"He passed out," Ned replied. "I don't know why. It's warm, but not that warm." He poured water on CJ's forehead. Then he poured more on his own bandanna and began gently swabbing CJ's face with the wet scarf. Finally his eyelids flickered and opened. "He's coming around," Ned said.

At that moment the other three riders turned around and came back from the road, where they were just about to start out.

"What happened to him?" Kendra asked in a worried voice, dismounting and kicking the stand on her bike into position. Her face was pale as she stared wide-eyed at CJ lying on the ground.

For the first time on the trip, Nancy felt some empathy for the girl who so easily antagonized people. She seemed to be genuinely concerned about CJ as she crouched down beside Nancy.

CJ managed a weak grin as he saw the circle of people around him. "Whew," he breathed, struggling to sit up. Ned slipped his arm behind him and gave him a boost. "Sorry about that," he said. "I don't know what hit me. I got these awful stomach cramps, and then I got really dizzy."

He looked up at the concerned faces around him, took a deep breath, and drew his knees up against his chest. But then he leaned forward as his face contorted with pain. "Cramps aren't gone yet," he said haltingly. "You guys go on. I'll catch up later." He struggled to his feet, wobbled, and then quickly sat down again, shaking his head as if to clear it.

"No way," said Ned. "We're not going to leave

you here. You can't even stand up. We should get you to a doctor." He looked around at the others. "Look, you folks go on. I'll stay with—" But his words were interrupted as George let out a scream and dropped to her knees to catch CJ just as he toppled backward.

"Water!" she said. "He's passed out again."

"This is serious," said Nancy. "We can't go anywhere until we get him some help. I haven't seen a car along here for two hours. Erik, will you ride back to the last town and phone for an ambulance?"

Erik nodded. "I'm on my way," he said, mounting up.

"Wait a minute!" Kendra reached out and gripped his handlebars as he was about to take off. She was shielding her eyes from the sun and staring in the direction from which they had ridden. Off in the distance, a vehicle was approaching. "I think that's Michael coming now. He was going to meet me here for lunch, but he must have been delayed. He can take CJ to a doctor."

George exchanged a glance with Nancy. "The first good idea she's had," she whispered.

Nancy nodded. "It *is* a good idea," she said. "He's really sick."

Jennifer, who had been standing on the edge of the circle, moved closer to them. "What's the matter with him? Do you know? Did he just pass out? Could it be food poisoning or something?"

"I don't think it's food poisoning, or we'd all have it," Nancy answered. "He said he had terrible cramps, and then he passed out." She turned to face Jennifer, whose concern for CJ was apparent. It was really true, Nancy thought, how an emergency could knit a group of bickering people together—sometimes. But why hadn't it happened when George had had her accident?

Kendra was standing almost in the middle of the road waving her arms at the approaching vehicle. Michael slowed the van, pulled off the road into the picnic area, and jumped out.

"What happened?" he called, peering at the cluster of people around CJ. "Another knee problem?"

"No, no. It's CJ. He's terribly sick. We have to get him to a doctor."

"CJ?"

"You know, the tall blond guy with glasses."

Michael nodded, and the two of them moved toward the group. Nancy watched his expression as he came closer. He seemed more puzzled by this emergency than surprised. A suspicious feeling crept over her, a sixth sense warning her to be alert. Was CJ's sudden illness caused by something they couldn't control? Or was it the result of someone's deliberate action?

Michael and Ned revived CJ, then supported him as he walked unsteadily to the van, where Erik was standing ready with the passenger door open. George, following close behind, wheeled CJ's bike up to the back doors.

"We passed a crossroad about a mile back," Ned told Michael. "If you go back to that road and take a left, there's a hospital in the first town you come to. Moorestown. I have a buddy who lives there. His father's one of the doctors, and he has an office in the hospital. Ask for Dr. Anderson."

"Gotcha. I know where Moorestown is," Michael replied, giving him a mock salute. He turned to George. "You want to go along for the ride, darlin'?" he asked, grinning at her. "I mean, I noticed that you and the patient are, well, special friends. We can just put your bike in the back, and you can ride along and play nurse."

George's eyes narrowed as she looked at him, and Nancy could tell that she was weighing the reason behind the offer. Before she could answer, Ned stepped in. "I'll ride along with CJ," he said. "I know a shortcut coming back. Then CJ and I can bike back together after he's been treated for whatever this is."

Without waiting for Michael to agree or disagree, Ned loaded his bike in the back with CJ's, then climbed into the seat behind Michael and CJ. The others in the group silently watched the van pull out, make a U-turn, and head back down the road. Even Kendra, who appeared to be irritated with Michael's offer to George, was subdued.

"Ready?" Erik said to George.

"I guess so." Her voice was strained, and Nancy could tell that she was worried. "I'm glad Ned went with him," she said to Nancy.

Erik glanced at the others. "Fayne and I are resuming the competition," he announced. "We'll see the three of you in about an hour, at the roadside park where we originally planned our afternoon break." He consulted his watch. "Even with the interruption, we still have plenty of daylight to get to our lodgings for the night."

They all put on their helmets. Then Erik and George rode off, and Nancy, Kendra, and Jennifer followed at a slower pace.

"That's so scary," Jennifer called to Nancy, who was riding a little ahead of her. "Just to have somebody pass out like that. Maybe he ate something that none of the rest of us did, something he had left over in his pack."

"Or he could have a heart condition that he didn't know about," Kendra volunteered, as they coasted down a slight incline. "Sometimes the healthiest people do. People you wouldn't suspect." She looked over at Nancy for confirmation.

"I'm sure they'll figure it out at the hospital," Nancy replied.

"I'm glad Ned went with him," Kendra continued. "It's so much better for him to have a guy along."

Nancy bit back a smile and thought of the

91

surprised look on Kendra's face when Michael had asked George to ride in the van. She concentrated on pedaling and didn't reply, concerned about CJ and hoping that he and Ned would be able to join them at the beautiful site where they were scheduled to spend the night.

She had been to Lakeview several years before with her father, at the height of the tourist season, and been captivated by the quiet beauty of the small lake with its sandy beach and the surrounding woods. The lake itself was dotted on one side with tiny cabins, built over the years by the owner, who lived in a spacious home on the grounds. While the cabins had a waiting list of vacationers during the summer months, the owner looked forward to the peaceful early weeks of fall, when the cycling groups came through and used the facilities. He not only lowered the rates for the students, but had become famous for the barbecue dinners he prepared for them in the huge stone fire pit that dominated a picnic area by the main house.

Jennifer and Kendra had pulled out ahead of her, and Nancy made no effort to catch up, glad to have some time alone to sort out her thoughts. Maybe she was overly suspicious about Jennifer. Maybe Jennifer was telling the truth about mailing her tuition payment. It could also be a coincidence that she and Palumbo worked at the same place. And while Kendra had undoubtedly written the note in a jealous huff, Nancy had no proof that she had trashed the room. Unlike their behavior when George had her accident, when Kendra had been accusatory and Jennifer had been silent, both girls had seemed genuinely concerned about CJ.

Nancy had to wonder where did Michael Kirby figure into all this. Why did he keep asking George to ride with him, when she had made it clear she wasn't interested in him? Why did he carry a gun in his van? And a file of newspaper accounts of the burglaries? Was it coincidence, or her own imagination, or was George really targeted for some reason?

And what about CJ's sudden illness? Could it have been food poisoning? But then, why didn't the rest of them get sick? They had all eaten the same food. Unless Jennifer was right and he had eaten some leftover food from his pack.

The late afternoon sun was warm. Nancy unclipped her water bottle, only to remember it was empty. She had given the water to Ned so he could revive CJ. She was clipping it back in place when the thought struck her. The water bottle! CJ's water bottle! No one else had drunk from it.

Nancy reached the roadside park a few minutes later. George was doing stretches, using a picnic table as a prop, and Erik was sitting across from her, eating an apple.

Nancy headed straight for George. "Got any water left?" she asked.

"Are you kidding?" George asked, picking up

her plastic bottle from the table and turning it upside down. "Not a drop."

"Let's go fill them," said Nancy, clutching her bottle.

"Now?" George asked. "I haven't finished my series."

Nancy raised an eyebrow. "Now," she said. Her voice was quiet and urgent.

"Oops!" said George. "I know that look. You're onto something. Something about CJ?" she asked as she followed Nancy toward the water fountain.

"I don't know yet," Nancy replied. "Remember this morning when Kendra was filling all the water bottles?"

George nodded.

"Did you get yours?"

George held out the bottle in her hand as proof. "Here it is."

"Are you sure it's yours?"

"Well, I think so. CJ and I have the same kind. Actually, half the cyclists in the world and I have the same kind. Except for the burn mark." She stopped walking to examine it, and a puzzled look crossed her face. "Nan," she continued. "Do you remember that camping trip I went on a couple of weeks ago?"

Nancy nodded.

"Well, my water bottle tipped over against a hot frying pan, and it melted a groove in the top.

This one doesn't have a mark on it. This is not my water bottle."

"That's what I was afraid of," Nancy said.

"What do you mean?" George asked.

"I think CJ has yours—and whatever made him sick was intended for you!"

Chapter

Eleven

GEORGE STARED at Nancy, shock apparent in her expression. "Then someone really *is* out to get me," she said. "But why? Oh, poor CJ. I feel so responsible for all this."

Nancy shook her head. "No way!" she said. "Whoever it is that's pulling these stunts has a reason, and I intend to find out who that person is. And since Kendra filled the water bottles, I think that's where I'll start."

"Are you going to talk to her now?" George asked, looking over at the trio standing by the bikes. "They're getting ready to pull out."

"No, not now," said Nancy. "We're not that far from Lakeview. I'll wait till we get there. I don't want to tip my hand in front of anyone else who might be a suspect." She gave George a frustrated look. "And unfortunately, at this point, they're *all* suspects."

"Well, if it's Erik, there's not much he can do to me while he's pumping that bike." She grinned. "He's not going to jeopardize his lead by taking time to bump me off while we're riding, so I guess I'll go and give him a run for his money. See you at the lake."

Despite her concern, Nancy smiled, too. "See you," she repeated. "By the way, we are sharing a cabin." She stressed the word *sharing*. "I'm sticking to you like glue when we get there."

The ride from the roadside stop to Lakeview was uneventful. Mr. Kipling, the owner, was waiting for them when they arrived. The wrinkles on his tanned face deepened into a smile as the cyclists approached. He was short, but there was nothing small about his bass voice. "Mr. Nickerson called from the hospital in Moorestown," he boomed. "Your friend is going to be all right. They're not sure what caused his collapse, but it's not his heart or anything major."

His announcement was greeted with comments of relief from all the riders. Nancy watched Kendra carefully while Mr. Kipling spoke. Her whole body, as well as her expression, seemed to relax after hearing the good news about CJ.

"I'd like a cabin by myself if possible," Jennifer said. She smiled shyly at the owner. She looked over at Kendra. "No offense intended, but my roommate has more of a social life than I do, and I'd like to get a good night's sleep before we start back."

"No problem," said Mr. Kipling. "Another cycling group just canceled their reservation. Each of you can have a private cabin if you want it." He handed out keys as he was talking.

"Just one for us," Nancy said. "George and I will share a cabin."

"Okay, then number ten for you two. It's a little bigger. You're all right in the same area. Your keys are numbered. Dinner's at seven," he continued. "Barbecued chicken. Come to the picnic area by the big house. The showers are over in that cement-block building." He laughed. "And our rustic communications center—that's the pay phone—is to the right of the showers, by the edge of the woods. The booth is a little rickety, but the phone works just fine."

"Thanks," Nancy said. "Let's go, George."

They wheeled their bikes over to cabin ten and unlocked the door. The cabin was sparsely furnished but neat and clean, with freshly laundered muslin curtains at the windows and a braided rag rug on the floor.

George stretched out on the bed. "I don't know what I want to do first," she said. "Take a nap or have a shower."

"They both sound good," Nancy agreed. She

had pulled the curtain aside from the window and was watching to see where the others were lodged. "Looks as if Kendra's got the place next to us, then Erik, and Jennifer's a couple down from him. She's closer to the woods."

"What did you think of her asking for a private cabin?" George asked, propping herself up on one elbow. "Isn't that a little strange, or am I getting paranoid?"

"I wondered myself, but it makes it easier for me to talk to Kendra alone," Nancy replied. "Jennifer's reason was legitimate. Kendra *did* come in late last night." She let the curtain drop. "Kendra's gone over to the showers. Why don't you go ahead and have a nap, and I'll talk to her when she comes back? Then we can go and clean up before dinner." Nancy turned around and smiled. George was already asleep.

Kendra was a long time in the shower building, and Nancy waited a few minutes after she came back, before going to her door. She was fairly certain what kind of a reception she was going to get, and she wasn't looking forward to it. George was still sleeping, and Nancy locked the cabin when she left.

She knocked lightly on the door to Kendra's cabin, and Kendra opened it immediately. She was dressed in sweats and barefooted, her face scrubbed clean of makeup and her head wrapped in a towel. "Come in," she said. "I've been expecting you."

99

Nancy, surprised at the comment, stepped inside. Kendra motioned for her to sit in the one chair in the room. She sat down on the edge of the bed, facing Nancy. Nancy could tell she'd been crying. Her face was puffy, and her eyes were red.

"You were responsible for CJ's illness," Nancy said to her. "Weren't you?"

Kendra nodded and covered her face with her hands. Her shoulders heaved up and down as she tried to catch her breath. "I'm sorry," she sobbed. "I never meant for him to get sick. I never meant for anybody to get *that* sick. Michael said it would just make a person throw up."

"You intended it for George," Nancy said.

"Yes, but—but somehow their water bottles got mixed up. And it wasn't my idea. It was Michael's. He was just trying to help me get even with her for being with CJ." She stopped and dug in her pocket for a tissue, then blew her nose loudly.

"Kendra, what did you put in that bottle? You could have killed someone!"

Kendra nodded. "I realized that when CJ kept passing out." She got up and walked over to the small desk at the foot of the bed and picked up a prescription bottle. "I take these antihistamines for allergies," she said, handing a bottle to Nancy. "And I take these," she said, handing her another bottle, "when I can't sleep. Before Michael and I went to the fair together, he saw them in my room. Later he said it would be a good way to put George out of commission for the rest of the ride. Just open up the capsules, one of each, and dump the stuff in her water bottle." She sniffled and blew her nose again.

"So you emptied the contents of the capsules into George's water bottle and then filled it up with all the others."

Kendra nodded. "Michael said the water at Bannon House was so heavily chlorinated that she'd never notice. But CJ picked up George's bottle. I didn't know it until he got sick."

Nancy stared at her in disbelief. She felt as if she were dealing with a child. "Kendra, don't you know anything about drug reactions? Didn't you realize that mixing two prescription drugs can be extremely dangerous? Or that someone might have an allergic reaction to the drugs?"

"Michael said it would just make her throw up," she repeated. "He even said everybody would blame Erik because he wants to beat George so badly. I'm sorry, Nancy. I'm truly sorry. I never meant for anything like this to happen."

"Kendra, I'm going to ask you a question, and I'd like a straight answer."

"Okay."

"Did you leave that note in our room last night?"

Kendra's gaze dropped to the floor. "Yes," she said quietly. "But I wasn't *in* your room. It was locked. I slipped the note under the door."

Nancy nodded. "Are you meeting Michael tonight?"

"He said he'd come by after dinner, but I'm not going anywhere with him. It was pretty dumb to go out with him in the first place—I mean, since I don't really know him and all. I was just so mad about George and CJ. . . ."

"I think that's a smart decision," Nancy replied. "When you do see him, I'd appreciate it if you didn't mention this conversation."

"Okay. Are you going to tell everybody that I put the stuff in the water?"

"No," Nancy said. "But I'll tell George. She deserves to know, since she was the target."

Kendra nodded. "Nancy?" she said hesitantly. "I called the hospital in Moorestown from here and told them what was in the water CJ drank. I didn't say who I was, though."

"At least you told them. That was the right thing to do."

Nancy left the cabin and walked back to hers. George was awake when she unlocked the door. "I'm still hungry and dirty, but I'm not tired now," she said. "How did you do with Kendra?"

"I'll tell you on the way to the showers."

Dinner was over when Michael arrived. "Folks at the hospital say they may keep CJ overnight," he announced as he approached the picnic area. "Nothing serious. Just stomach upset. Nickerson's going to stay with him." He seemed disappointed that his good news had been preceded by a phone call with the same information.

Nancy leaned over to George. "This is a good time to split," she said quietly, getting up. They were walking back to their cabin when Mr. Kipling came out of the main house, carrying a guitar and a big bag of marshmallows.

"Oh, you're not leaving already?" he said. "I've got a bonfire going down on the beach."

"We're pretty tired, Mr. Kipling," Nancy said. "But the others are still at the table."

"Well, goodnight then."

George smiled. "It's like a personal insult to him if you leave early. Come to think of it, Nancy, why are we leaving early?"

"Because we have work to do."

"That's what I was afraid of. I thought that with Kendra's confession, we had this all figured out. Who are we working on now?"

"Jennifer. We still haven't figured out who cut your brake cables. Or who trashed our room last night. Or why Jennifer was looking for a bus. I want to check her room while she's down on the beach."

"Okay," said George. "But I guarantee you're not going to find anything in her room. She carries it all with her. I think that hot-pink fanny pack of hers is like a growth around her waist.

You never see her without it. I'll bet she sleeps with it on!"

Nancy grinned and pulled something out of the pocket of her jeans. "Maybe." She stopped at the door to Jennifer's cabin, slid the credit card in her hand between the doorjamb and the lock, then slowly turned the knob. The door opened. "Set that small table lamp on the floor," she said to George. "And cover it with a pillowcase. It'll give us enough light to see by but won't be obvious from the beach."

George nodded. "I'll take the backpack," she said. "You take the stuff on the desk."

"Look!" said Nancy, moving over toward the light. "Her wallet and her checkbook. If she left this stuff here, I wonder what she does carry in that fanny pack." She handed the checkbook to George. "See what's in here while I look in the billfold."

"Wow!" George said. "She's had two hefty deposits in the last thirty days, two hundred dollars each, about ten days apart. She can't earn *that* much working part-time at the diner. And from what she told us, her parents couldn't send her this much money. Oh, this is interesting," George continued. "She spent fifty bucks at a beauty parlor on Friday."

"This is interesting, too," Nancy said, as she examined the contents of Jennifer's wallet. "How tall are you, George?"

"Five feet eight inches, as if you didn't know."

"Color of hair?"

"What do you mean, color of hair?"

"Color of eyes?"

"What is this, Nancy? Twenty questions?"

Nancy laughed. "Look here," she said, passing the wallet to George. "Look at her driver's license. At a quick glance, who does that picture remind you of?"

George held the license out at arm's length and looked at it critically. "The haircut's the same, and she's definitely a natural brunette." She looked up at Nancy. A sense of foreboding passed between them as each stared at the other.

"Nan," George said, "do you think somebody's mistaking me for Jennifer?"

Chapter
Twelve

IT'S POSSIBLE," Nancy said. "Someone who doesn't really know Jennifer or someone who saw her when her hair was its natural color and combed this way. There's a definite resemblance between the two of you."

"Well, the color change explains the fifty-dollar check to the beauty shop," George said.

"When did you say that was written?" Nancy asked, frowning.

"Friday. The day before yesterday. Why?"

"I was wondering why she'd have her hair color changed the day before a bike trip," Nancy said. "I could understand if she were going to a dance or a party or something—but for a bike trip? It doesn't make sense. Unless she had it done as a disguise, instead of just for vanity." Nancy looked closely at George. "You know, you

106

are built the same. In fact, when I saw her standing at the window in the lounge on Friday night, I mistook her for you."

George nodded. "And remember on Saturday morning, Erik made some comment about her hair. Like he was seeing her as a blond for the first time. But they had classes together on Friday, I think. So she must have had her hair bleached Friday night. Which would explain why she didn't go to work." She paused and scratched her head. "Which explains what?"

Nancy shrugged. "Maybe nothing. Maybe she just wanted a change. But whatever it means, she *used* to resemble you in a general way."

"Poor thing," George quipped. "Same shape, same coloring, same build, but lucky for her, she doesn't have my face!"

"Cut it out, George," Nancy said. Her expression changed from a grin to a puzzled frown. "I think that your resemblance to Jennifer might explain your series of accidents."

"You mean somebody's after Jennifer?" The surprise in George's voice was apparent.

Nancy looked up at her friend. "It's possible. We have to figure out why. When did she make those deposits?"

George flipped through the pages of the check register and read off two dates, as Nancy jotted them down on a scrap of paper. "And there's a *third* two-hundred-dollar deposit that she made on Wednesday."

Nancy studied the information and shook her head. "I can't figure out the significance," she said. "Look, you go through her backpack and see if you find anything suspicious. I'm going to call the Emersonville police."

"Okay," George replied. She walked to the window and pulled aside the curtain and squinted into the night. "There's a light in the phone booth, but that's about all I can see. What if the party breaks up? I'll need some warning to get out of here."

"I'll be able to see them from the booth," Nancy said, "especially since there's a bonfire. If they start coming toward the cabins, I'll whistle. That means get out."

"Got it," said George. She already had Jennifer's backpack unzipped and was systematically laying things out on the floor as she searched through the contents.

Nancy closed the door firmly behind her, and the lock clicked. After a cautious glance around, she jogged quietly toward the phone booth. She could hear the soft sounds of the group singing as she dialed the number. A woman officer, Sergeant Telfer, answered the call.

"This is Nancy Drew," she said. "Is Lieutenant Easterling still around?"

"No, Ms. Drew, he left around dinnertime. But he told me you'd be calling. Let me see what I've got here." There was a brief pause. "First of all, he wanted you to know that we did finally get hold of the judge, and we got a search warrant for Palumbo's place."

"Did you find the rest of the stuff?" Nancy asked.

"Not a thing," said the sergeant. "His place was clean as a whistle."

"Which means it's almost certain that he's passing on the stolen goods to a fence," Nancy said.

"That's what we figure. But we haven't been able to link him to anyone, and he's not volunteering anything."

"Lieutenant Easterling was trying to get some information for me from the authorities in Florida," Nancy continued. "Do you have it?"

Sergeant Telfer cleared her throat. "I hate to keep giving you negative news," she said, "but we don't have anything yet. They've got the tail end of a hurricane going through down there, and their computer system went down. I phoned them about an hour ago, and they said they should be back on-line soon. Can I call you as soon as the information comes in?"

Nancy bit her lower lip. What rotten luck. "No," she said. "I'm at a pay phone in the middle of nowhere. I'd better call you back."

"Okay. Give them about an hour. I should have something for you by then. Oh, and Ms. Drew?"

"Yes."

"Lieutenant Easterling is worried about you. He said to tell you to be careful."

"Thanks," Nancy said. "I appreciate his concern, and I *am* being careful. I do have one more question for you," Nancy continued. "It's kind of off-the-wall, though."

"Try me," the sergeant said, laughing. "It can't be any more off-the-wall than some I've fielded in this job."

Nancy smiled at her good humor. "Have you ever heard of a beauty shop in Emersonville called Cassie's Crowning Glory?"

"Heard of it?" The officer chuckled. "Cassie gets a chunk of my paycheck every month."

"Great!" Nancy said. "Not about your paycheck," she added quickly. "About my question. Do you know if Cassie's shop is open evenings? Like, would she be open Friday nights?"

"Maybe not regularly," the woman answered. "But Cassie's pretty flexible. Her shop's in her home. She pretty much opens up any time that anyone wants to have her hair done. She's a widow. Not many demands on her time, except for her customers."

Nancy's thoughts were whirling as Sergeant Telfer talked. That meant that Jennifer could have had her hair bleached on Friday night. And she could have made a spur-of-the-moment decision to do it, which would explain why she had called in sick to work at the last minute and why

Erik had made a comment about her hair on Saturday morning.

"One more question," Nancy said. "Can you give me the dates of the previous burglaries?"

"Easy," said the officer. "They're burned into my memory."

Nancy squinted at the scrap of paper in her hand as Sergeant Telfer quickly cited the dates. Each deposit in Jennifer's account came two or three days after each of the three burglaries, previous to the Friday night break in. Was it coincidence, or was there a pattern that would link Jennifer Bover to the Emersonville burglaries?

"Are you still there, Ms. Drew?"

The woman's voice brought Nancy back from her thoughts.

"Yes, sorry. I was just checking those dates against some bank deposits made by Jennifer Bover. She's one of the riders on our bike trip."

"Bover," the sergeant repeated. "She's someone Lieutenant Easterling checked on for you, right?"

"Right," said Nancy. "But there was nothing on her. Look, would you do me a favor? He offered to check Bover with the campus police, and I told him it wouldn't be necessary."

"Change your mind?" the officer asked.

"Yes," Nancy said. "Could you please see if they have anything on her?"

"Sure. I'd be glad to."

The beam of a flashlight on the slope caught Nancy's attention, and she stretched the metal-coil phone cord to its limit as she leaned out for a better look. The singing had stopped, and in the glow from the fire, she could see figures outlined as they walked up the hill.

"I've got to go!" Nancy said urgently. "I'll call back." She slammed the receiver back on the hook and gave a loud piercing whistle as she glanced toward Jennifer's cabin. She saw that it was dark. George must have already left, she thought.

Nancy shoved the scrap of paper into the pocket of her jeans and stepped outside the booth. As she did, there was a crackling of leaves behind the phone booth and the sound of footsteps.

Someone was running toward the woods. And, Nancy realized, that person must have been hiding nearby, listening to her conversation!

Chapter

Thirteen

N ANCY ROUNDED the booth to chase the eaves-dropper, but the person had already disappeared into the trees. How much had the person heard? Did the person know she had been talking to the police? She glanced back over her shoulder. The people coming up the hill had drifted off to their cabins, but another figure was running toward her. George! What was she doing out here?

"To your left!" George yelled.

She must have seen the person, too, as she was coming out of Jennifer's cabin. Between the two of them, maybe they could cut him or her off.

As Nancy ran, her sneakers kept sliding on the slippery pine needles. Just as Nancy ducked under a low-hanging branch and veered to the left, she heard a thud. She stopped and turned.

George had fallen! Nancy changed direction immediately and ran to her friend.

"Oh, rats," George wailed. She was sitting on the ground, hugging one leg, which was bent at the knee. The other was stretched straight out in front of her. "I can't believe how stupid I am!" She boosted herself up, putting her weight on one leg, and winced. "That stupid root or whatever it was. I didn't even see it."

"Of course you couldn't see it," Nancy said, quickly putting her arm around George's waist to support her. "It's dark, and it was covered with pine needles. Can you walk?"

"I'm not sure," George said. "Talk about a big-time klutz. We almost had that person." Gingerly she put her weight on the sore leg.

"I'm going to get Mr. Kipling," Nancy said.

"No," George said. "Just give me a hand back to the cabin."

Nancy nodded. "Okay. Drape your arm over my shoulder. We'll take it slow. Did you find anything in Jennifer's room?"

"No." George shook her head. "Nothing. I was out of there before they started back up from the beach. I was coming to get you when I heard you whistle. I thought I saw something, so I hid in that clump of bushes over there. That's when I saw him running."

"Or her," said Nancy.

"Or her," George repeated.

Supported by her friend, George half hopped, half hobbled back to their cabin.

"I'll be fine in a few minutes," she said, sitting down on the bed.

"I'm going over to the big house to get you some ice," Nancy said. "And I'm locking you in."

George nodded her thanks. "That'll help more than anything," she said. "The ice, not being locked in, I mean." She gingerly reached forward and circled the sore knee with both hands. "It hasn't started to swell," she said. "Maybe it won't. Nancy, could you tell who it was?"

"No," Nancy replied. "We'll talk when I get back. I'll hurry."

"Watch yourself out there," George cautioned, but Nancy was already out of the cabin. George heard the lock click.

When Nancy returned with a plastic bowl full of ice, George was sitting in a chair by the window, with her leg propped up on another chair. She had a towel in her hands.

"Do you have any idea who it was?" George asked Nancy again, as she put the ice in the towel, then wrapped it around her knee. "Was it a man or a woman?"

"I don't know," said Nancy. "And I don't know how long the person was there. I didn't realize anyone was listening until I went to leave the booth."

"Probably overheard your whole conversation," George said morosely. "What did you find out?"

"Not much," said Nancy. "The information from Florida hasn't come in yet. The place where Jennifer got her hair done is open Friday nights, and each of the big deposits in her checking account was made a couple of days after the three other Emerson burglaries. Which isn't exactly evidence of guilt. But . . ."

"But what?" George asked.

"But I have a hunch that somehow Jennifer is connected." She looked over at George and waved her hands in a frustrated gesture. "I just don't want to believe it of her, I guess. She doesn't seem like the type to be mixed up in anything criminal."

"I know," George agreed. "She seems so wholesome. I mean, showing off that picture of her brothers and sisters. You can tell she really cares about her family."

Nancy nodded. "Yes, and kids seem to gravitate to her, like those little boys on the swings at lunchtime yesterday."

"And I heard her trying to talk Kendra into doing volunteer work with her at the Women's Shelter on Saturday afternoons."

Nancy sighed. "Dad says that often the ones who appear to be most innocent are the most guilty. I just hate to think Jennifer's mixed up in anything bad."

George sat up straighter and leaned over to peer out the window. "Somebody's coming up the path."

Nancy turned off the light and joined her at the window. "It must be Erik," she said. "He stayed down at the beach after the others left to help Mr. Kipling clean up. They were coming back when I went to get the ice."

A door slammed, and then a light went on inside Erik's cabin, showing him clearly.

George sighed. "I guess that lets him out as an eavesdropping suspect," she said. "Even the great Erik can't be in two places at once."

Nancy nodded. "Right. And after our talk today, I don't think it was Kendra. She was very frank with me. She wouldn't have any reason to eavesdrop on a phone call. By the way, since you're the designated peeping Tom, has she come back to her cabin yet?"

"Home and probably all tucked in by now," George reported. "Michael walked her to the door while you were getting ice, and then took off."

Nancy nodded. "I noticed that his van was gone," she said.

George gingerly stretched her leg out and shifted the ice pack. "This is feeling a little better," she said. "I'm going to try to put my weight on it." She stood up and took a few cautious steps. "Not bad. Not great, but not bad." She turned to face Nancy, who was still standing at the window, looking out. "Nan, if you've ruled out Kendra and Erik, that leaves us with Michael and Jennifer."

Nancy nodded, without turning her head. "Take a look at this," she said, motioning to George.

George moved cautiously to the window and followed Nancy's gaze. In the moonlight a solitary figure was moving stealthily away from the cabins toward the wooded area.

"It's Jennifer," Nancy whispered. "I'm going to follow her. Keep the light off."

"Keep the light off?" George repeated, dramatically looking around. "Who are you talking to? I'm going with you!"

"Not with that knee," Nancy said.

"But we're not running this time," said George. "We're sneaking. And my knee is always up to sneaking."

"Sorry," Nancy said firmly. "I'm going solo. I won't be long. Stand guard." She opened the cabin door and exited before George could answer.

The light in Erik's cabin went off as Nancy passed by. The rest of the units were already dark. Nancy stayed a safe distance from Jennifer, taking care not to make any noise in the loose underbrush as she entered the woods. The moon, covered intermittently by slow-moving clouds, provided enough light for her to watch, as Jennifer stopped in a small clearing, crouched down, and began to dig. She had the small shovel from the barbecue pit, and it was clear to Nancy that she was burying something. But what?

She watched in silence as the blond girl took something from her fanny pack, placed it in the hole she had dug, covered it with dirt, and carefully brushed pine needles over it. Then she reached for a rock and planted it to one side of the burial site. After looking furtively around, she straightened up and hurried back to the path that led to the cabins.

Nancy waited until she heard the door to Jennifer's cabin close before she moved into the woods. Unsure whether someone else might be lurking nearby, Nancy looked around warily, her ears straining for any foreign sounds in the hush of the night. Finally satisfied that she was alone, she took the rock that had been left as a marker and used it to scoop out the soft dirt, uncovering a small felt bag with a drawstring closure.

Nancy pulled the drawstring open and dumped the contents of the pouch into her palm. Her breath caught in her throat, and she stared in disbelief.

"The emeralds," Nancy whispered, staring at the glittering jewelry. "The stolen emeralds."

Chapter

Fourteen

Nancy stood up slowly, the jewelry still clutched in her hand. She felt as if someone had punched her in the stomach.

She was beginning to understand the reasons behind the accidents of the past forty-eight hours, but she was disappointed. She had hoped that Jennifer was not involved. That possibility was now out of the question. She slipped the jewels back into the pouch, pushed the pouch into her jacket pocket, and slowly walked back to the cabin.

"Well?" said George expectantly, turning on the lamp as Nancy softly closed the door behind her and locked it.

"Well," said Nancy, reaching into her pocket, "she was burying this." She opened the pouch and took out the emerald jewelry.

George gasped. "Can I see them?" she whispered, reaching out and picking up the necklace from Nancy's hand. "This is gorgeous." She held it up. Even in the dim lamplight, the expensive stones glittered with rays of green. The center square-cut gem was flanked by four other square-cut emeralds, smaller in size but equal in brilliance, set in gold filigree. The matching bracelet had six graduated emeralds and fastened with a gold clasp. Each of the delicate drop earrings consisted of three tiny gems, strung on gold chains. "They must be worth a fortune," George said.

"Fifty thousand," Nancy replied. "And Lieutenant Easterling said they're heirlooms."

She slipped the earrings and bracelet into the soft cloth bag and held it open for George, who carefully slid in the necklace. Nancy pulled the drawstring taut, tucked the pouch into her jacket pocket, then peered out the window into the night. "I have a feeling that we may not have been the only ones who had an eye on Jennifer."

"Possible," George replied. She leaned over and turned off the light. "Now we know why Jennifer wore that fanny pack all the time. She was carrying the emeralds in it."

Nancy nodded. "Yes, and the emeralds may have been the reason she was looking for a post office, too. But where would she mail them? She knows that Palumbo's in jail."

"Maybe she was going to mail them to herself," George suggested.

"Good thought," Nancy acknowledged.

"And since she couldn't get to a post office," George continued, "she thought she'd catch a bus and run away with them."

"That doesn't hold up," Nancy said. "She could have left Emerson with them as early as Wednesday. They came from a burglary Monday night."

George nodded. "I guess you're right," she said. "I know this sounds crazy, but do you actually think that Jennifer is the fence for Palumbo? I mean, we know that she knows him, but how would she know where to peddle stolen jewelry? Or anything else, for that matter. She's a college student majoring in early childhood education. Not exactly top qualifications for a jewelry fence."

Despite the seriousness of the situation, Nancy smiled. "I just don't have the answer to that," she said. "Yet."

"So what do we do now?"

"I'm going to call Sergeant Telfer again. The police need to know that we've recovered the emeralds. And the report from Florida might shed some light on this, if it's in. You're going to stay here with the door locked and the lights out and watch for any activity around the cabins."

"And guard the emeralds," George added.

"No," said Nancy. "The emeralds are going with me."

"That's not fair," George protested. "You're setting yourself up as a target. If you won't leave them here, at least let me go along to protect you."

"George," Nancy said gently. "You're the one who needs protection. You see, if someone is after these emeralds, whoever it is is looking for a young woman who's tall and has dark hair. Jennifer used to look like that before she had her hair bleached. You fit the description. But I don't. The emeralds go with me."

"I never thought of that," George mumbled. She sat down on the side of the bed. "Nan, be careful out there."

Nancy nodded. "I will. I promise. If you see Jennifer leaving her cabin, whistle at me. If you see *anything,* whistle at me!"

"Okay."

"When I come back, I'll knock twice, and then twice again. That way you'll know it's me."

Nancy pulled the door firmly shut behind her and listened for the lock to catch before she started down the path to the phone booth. Off in the woods to her left she could hear the plaintive hoot of an owl, the only sound to break the silence of the night. With one hand in her jacket pocket, she fingered the soft fabric pouch that protected the emeralds, and tried to visualize the women who'd worn them and the occasions on which they'd been worn.

She glanced back up at their dark cabin, where she knew George was watching at the window, and a vague feeling of uneasiness came over her. She'd be glad when the bike trip was over and they were safely home. Nancy sighed. One thing was certain. George was in grave danger.

She gave one final look around and stepped into the phone booth. Headquarters answered on the second ring, and within moments Nancy was connected with Sergeant Telfer.

"I thought you were never going to get back to me," the officer said as soon as Nancy identified herself. Without waiting for Nancy to reply, she continued. "I called the lieutenant about the Florida report as soon as I read it." Sergeant Telfer's voice was tense with excitement. "Ms. Drew, you are in imminent danger. The lieutenant says you are to take every precaution if the man you know as Michael Kirby joins your group again. He also goes by the name Kirby Stanton, and he's wanted by the police in four states, including this one and Florida."

"Kirby Stanton," Nancy repeated. "K.S. Those were the initials on the briefcase in his van."

"He has a long record of vehicular theft, assault, and armed robbery, and must be"—she repeated the words—"*must be* considered armed and dangerous. Do you understand?"

"Yes," Nancy replied. "I understand. He left the campground an hour ago. But I'll be careful. Does he have any connection with Stephen Palumbo?"

"Yes, he and Palumbo served time together in Florida, and we think they were partners in three jewelry store robberies in Texas. Texas authorities think Stanton was the fence, but they couldn't prove it."

"The fence!" Nancy said. "So it's probable that he's the fence for Palumbo in the Emersonville burglaries, too." She paused and then spoke, almost to herself. "So where does Jennifer fit in?"

"I don't know," Sergeant Telfer said. "We believe Kirby Stanton's the fence, but Palumbo hasn't admitted it."

"Sergeant, I have the emeralds from one of the Emersonville burglaries." Nancy could hear the woman gasp on the other end of the line. "It's a long and complicated story," Nancy continued, "but I think that's what Michael Kirby, or Kirby Stanton, is looking for. They were in the possession of Jennifer Bover, one of the cyclists. Were the campus police able to give you anything more on her?"

"Nothing. A clean sheet. But having the emeralds would certainly implicate her." The sergeant's no-nonsense voice became even more stern. "I have your itinerary in front of me, but I want you to tell me exactly where you are, so we can get a car over there to give you some protection."

"Right," said Nancy. "I'm in cabin ten at Kipling's Lakeview Lodge, just off County Road Thirty-three."

"Good," said Sergeant Telfer. "Go back to your cabin and lock yourself in. Now that you have those emeralds, you are a definite target for Stanton, and possibly Bover, too. They may be working against each other, and you could get caught in the crossfire. The nearest police force is in Moorestown. We'll radio them to get over there. What is Stanton driving?"

"A blue van. I gave Lieutenant Easterling the license number and model yesterday."

Nancy could hear papers rustling as the woman checked the file.

"Here it is. It checked out to a rental agency. I'll put out an APB. We'll get someone over there as soon as possible." Her voice softened. "Nancy —be careful."

"Thanks," Nancy replied. "I will."

She sighed and replaced the receiver. Things were starting to fall into place. Palumbo and Stanton, alias Michael Kirby, were working together, with Palumbo pulling off the burglaries and Stanton selling the goods. But where did Jennifer Bover fit in? College student. Early childhood education major. No criminal record.

Nancy shoved her hands into the pockets of her jacket and closed her fingers around the felt bag that held the emeralds. It was getting colder. The wind was coming in off the lake now, and the sky was clouding over. She glanced at the cabins. They were all dark. She walked slowly up the path, the crunching sound of her sneakers on the loose gravel the only noise in the night. Her whole body was tense, alert, but there was no sign of life around the campground. She'd be glad to get inside, share the new information with George, and wait for the police from Moorestown to arrive. She hadn't realized she was so tired.

Nancy stopped outside the cabin she was sharing with George and listened. Nothing. She lifted her hand and gently knocked twice. Waited. Knocked twice again.

There was a click as George turned the lock and opened the door. Nancy stepped inside, her eyes squinting against the dark interior.

"Close the door quietly, Ms. Drew."

Michael Kirby stepped from the shadows into her line of vision. His left arm was wrapped around George's neck and his right hand held a gun to her temple!

Chapter

Fifteen

GEORGE!"

Nancy stepped toward them, staring with horror as Kirby's grip tightened around George's neck.

"Keep your distance," Kirby warned menacingly, "or I'll shoot her. Now take the emeralds out of your pocket." He smirked at Nancy's look of surprise. "Yes, I know what you've got and where you've got them."

"He knew because he was outside the cabin listening to us before you went to make the call," George blurted out defiantly. "He even knew the knock signal. That's why I let him in."

"Shut up!" Kirby snapped. "Put them on the table." Pulling George with him, he moved a few steps to the table and, without letting go of the gun, picked up the pouch and slipped it into his pocket. "Okay, ladies, now we're going to go for a ride. Don't try any tricks, Ms. Private Eye. You're going to lead. And remember, I've got this gun wedged right into your friend's waist."

"You won't get away with this, Kirby," Nancy said. "The police are on their way here now."

"Right," he replied sarcastically. "And if they're anything like the Emersonville cops, they might find the place in two days. Besides, your friend here doesn't want to see them any more than I do. She'll have a bit of explaining to do."

"I told you before and I'll tell you again, you've got the wrong person!" George snapped.

"Give me a break," Kirby replied. "You're the wrong person, but you just happen to have the emeralds, right?

"You didn't know that I saw you on one of the drops, did you? Wearing those big sunglasses at five in the morning. What a disguise!" He gave a sarcastic laugh. "Once I see somebody, I don't forget them. The hair, the shape, the walk. I knew it was you the minute I"—he paused to sneer at her—"just 'happened' to find your cycling group. Convenient that you told the restaurant people that you were going on a bike trip this weekend, or I might still be looking over the Emerson coeds trying to find you. When I realized you'd kept back the emeralds on that Wednesday drop, I knew I'd have to go after you. It was good of the local press to tell me what was missing."

"But she's not the drop person! She's telling you the truth," Nancy said. "She's not even an Emerson student."

"Well I'd check that out with Palumbo if I could, but we both know that he's not in a position to give me any more information. And frankly, the only reason she was involved in the first place was so he and I wouldn't have to make contact. It would have been—how shall I put it?—it would have been dangerous for us."

"They already know you're involved with Palumbo, and they know you're the fence for the Texas robberies, too, Kirby Stanton," Nancy said. "You're only making it worse for yourself."

His eyes narrowed as she said the name *Stanton*. "Save your breath," he said. "It doesn't matter whether she's the drop or not. I've got what I want. In twenty-four hours I'll be in Canada, and these emeralds are going to buy me a whole new identity. Now, open the door, Ms. Private Eye, turn left, walk through that grove of trees, and we'll be right behind you."

"You'll never make it to Canada," Nancy said.

"Move it!" Kirby snapped. "And no noise or your friend gets it."

Having no choice, Nancy did as she was ordered. The van was parked on a dirt trail on the far side of the grove, hidden from the campground. Kirby yanked open the driver's door.

"You're driving," he said to Nancy. "The keys are in the ignition. You're going to follow this trail to a concession road. No lights and no tricks, or your friend gets it. Understand?"

Nancy's heart sank. She didn't even know a back road existed, and she didn't know where it went. The police would be looking for them at the cabin or on the county road.

Kirby shoved George roughly into the passenger seat beside Nancy and climbed into the seat behind them, placing the gun to the base of George's head. "Any swerves, any signals, any fancy driving, and I kill your friend. Got it?"

Nancy nodded. The moon shining through the tall trees gave barely enough light to see the trail. She was sure Kirby meant every threat he made, and she wasn't about to endanger George. Their only hope would be if the Moorestown police used this road as a shortcut to reach Lakeview Lodge. That hope faded quickly when Kirby had her pull off the dirt trail and turn on the headlights.

The road was poorly maintained and obviously little traveled. No oncoming lights were visible, and checking the rearview mirror, Nancy saw no traffic following them. Behind her, she could hear Kirby fumbling for something in the dark, but a quick glance in the mirror confirmed that the gun was still held at George's head.

"Here," he muttered to George. "Put this in your pocket." He reached over the seat and handed something to George.

Nancy looked over to see what it was.

"I don't get it," George said, looking at the emerald drop earring Kirby had given her.

"You don't have to get it," he snarled. "Just do what you're told."

"I guess I'm not in a position to argue," George said angrily, jamming the earring into the pocket of her jeans.

"You've got that right!" said Kirby. As he spoke he lifted the gun and hit George on the side of the head. She slumped over, her cheek against the door frame.

Nancy slammed the brakes. "You beast!" she yelled.

Kirby laughed and almost casually slid over behind her. She felt the cold muzzle of the revolver behind her ear and froze in place.

"Now, is that any way to talk to me?" he asked in a soft voice. "Take your foot off the brake and move this buggy down the road. Do what you're told, and nothing will happen to you."

"You're insane!"

"Keep it moving. Your friend's going to have a little nap for the next few miles, and then we're going to dispose of her."

Nancy gripped the wheel tightly and looked over at George. She was out cold. What else did he have planned for them?

As if he was reading her mind, Kirby responded. "About three miles down, there's a bend in the road, and around the bend there's a small bridge over a creek. When you get across the bridge, pull over to the shoulder."

Nancy scanned the road ahead of her. No traffic. Not even a farmhouse in sight. It was like being in the middle of nowhere. Would the police ever find them, and when they did, would it be too late?

"We're coming up to the bend," Kirby snapped, interrupting her thoughts.

"You can't get away with this," Nancy said, as she slowed for the curve. "Don't you have any conscience? George wasn't involved at all."

"But she's involved now," Kirby said. "And when they find her, she'll have part of the loot in her pocket." He laughed. "I've got this all worked out. The police will think she was the fence, who was robbed and killed on a back road while escaping to Canada with the emeralds. Unfortunately, in their rush to get the jewels, her assailants missed one of the earrings."

"What about the woman who *was* the drop?" Nancy asked, stalling for time.

"What about her? She's not going to come forward and confess."

"What about Palumbo? He could cut a deal with the police that would put you behind bars."

"Not likely," Kirby replied curtly. "I know too much about Stephen Palumbo. If he squeals on me, he's looking at a lot more than a burglary charge." He hit the back of the seat with his hand

and Nancy jumped. "You're too nosy," he said. "Stop! Right here."

Nancy pulled the van over and cut the engine. Her mind was racing. Was he going to kill George right here at the side of the road? How was she going to get out of this? Keep him talking, she told herself. Maybe someone will come along.

"What are you going to do with me?" she asked, in as cool a tone as she could muster. "Obviously I'm not involved in the burglaries. How are you going to explain my body at the side of the road?"

Kirby laughed—a hideous laugh that sent shivers up Nancy's spine. "You're not going to be left at the side of the road, my dear. At least not here. You see, your friend's usefulness is over. But you are still an asset to me."

"I don't see how," Nancy said.

"I thought you'd be smart enough to figure that out," Kirby replied. "If the police really are looking for me—and I'm not sure I believe you on that—then they're looking for a single man, not for a couple headed for a vacation in Canada."

As he talked, Nancy's hands tightened on the steering wheel. Her palms were clammy, and she could feel beads of perspiration on her forehead.

"It's time," Kirby said flatly. "Get out. And don't try anything stupid. I'm getting out on your side, so I'll be right behind you. And don't forget I still have this." He stroked the gun over the hair at her neck. "And I won't hesitate to use it if I have to. Open your door."

As if programmed, the two of them got out of the van in tandem. The minute Nancy's feet hit the ground, Kirby grabbed her arm, keeping the revolver trained on her.

"Now we'll walk around the van together," he instructed. "You'll open the door and pull your friend over to the edge of that ditch."

Nancy's heart was pounding. She had to do something, but what? They walked to the passenger side of the van, and Nancy reached out and opened the door. George's limp body slid into her arms, and she half carried, half dragged her from the vehicle to a grassy strip by the ditch.

"Say goodbye," Kirby said. Nancy felt his muscular arm curl around her neck from behind. Holding her tightly in front of him, he raised the gun and aimed it at George's head. The click as he released the safety catch resounded like a thunderbolt in Nancy's ears.

Chapter

Sixteen

THE CLICK OF THE safety on the revolver jarred Nancy to action. Kirby was holding her tightly in front of him, his left arm wrapped around her shoulders in a bruising grip. Fiercely Nancy jabbed backward with her elbow. The unexpected blow caught Kirby in the stomach. He flung his arm up in the air, and the shot went wild.

Kirby doubled over in pain, and Nancy whirled around and disarmed him with a quick chop to the wrist. As he straightened up, raging, she caught him under the chin with a high kick. He staggered backward and fell, just as the lights of a vehicle rounded the bend and crossed the bridge. The police! Two officers jumped out of the black-and-white patrol car and ran toward her.

"Are you all right?" one asked while the other ran over to Kirby, who was struggling to get up, and handcuffed him.

"Yes, I'm okay," Nancy said, running over to George. "But my friend is hurt. I'm Nancy Drew, by the way."

"I'll call for an ambulance," he yelled, charging back to the car.

Nancy knelt beside George and held her hand. She was still unconscious, but her breathing seemed normal. Nancy was concentrating so hard on George that she scarcely noticed the truck that pulled up behind the police car until she heard a familiar voice calling her.

"Nan!"

She looked up. "Over here! Oh, Ned, I'm so glad to see you."

Ned, with CJ close behind, ran over to where she was kneeling by George.

"Kirby hit her in the head with his gun," Nancy said. "We need to get her to a doctor."

"I saw some plywood in the back of the truck," CJ said. He ran back to the side of the road and returned soon with a long piece of plywood and a blanket.

"Excuse me, Ms. Drew," said one of the officers. "We need to get a statement from you."

"Where are you taking him?" she asked, nodding toward Kirby.

"The county jail in Moorestown," he replied.

"Can I meet you there?" Nancy asked. "We

need to get my friend to the clinic right away. We'll take her in. Cancel the ambulance."

"All right. Follow us. We'll escort you."

Ned and CJ had covered George with the blanket and were carrying her to the truck on the makeshift stretcher.

"Wait a minute," Nancy said to the officers. "How did you find us? This road is totally deserted."

"We would have been out on the county road if it hadn't been for your friend back at the lodge," one of them replied.

Nancy's brow furrowed. "Mr. Kipling?"

"No, no. The young woman—tall, blond. She apparently saw Kirby taking you and your friend to the van, and she followed on her bike. She watched him turn onto this side road. So when we got to the lake, she told us which way to go." He paused. "If it hadn't been for her, we would have gone in the wrong direction." He touched the brim of his cap in a brief salute. "Well, we'll see you in Moorestown."

Jennifer, Nancy said to herself, after he left. Jennifer had told the Moorestown police how to find them. Why? Before the night was over, the police were going to learn that she was working with Kirby and Palumbo. Nancy shook her head. She would have to sort things out later.

She hurried to the truck. "CJ," she said, "I'm sorry I ignored you. I was so worried about George. How are you feeling?"

"I'm fine," he said, patting her shoulder.

"I'll get into the back with George," Nancy said. Ned and CJ got into the front, and Ned started the motor and pulled out behind the police car.

CJ looked back over his shoulder at Nancy. "How's she doing?"

"The same," Nancy replied.

"Was Kirby responsible for my trip to the hospital, too?"

"Partly," Nancy said. "The idea was his. Kendra actually put the drugs in the bottle. The water was intended for George."

"Will somebody please tell me what's going on?" Ned said. "I feel as if I've come into a bad movie about an hour late."

Nancy laughed. "I'll tell you what's been happening here, if you'll tell me where you found this truck."

"That's easy," Ned replied. "CJ and I biked over from Moorestown after they released him from the hospital, and we got to the lodge about the same time as the police. When we figured out that they were looking for Kirby and Kirby was gone and that you and George were gone too, we decided we'd better follow them. Mr. Kipling couldn't stand to see two grown men wailing about their lost loves, so he loaned us his truck."

"Ned, you are certifiably crazy!" Nancy said.

* * *

THE NANCY DREW FILES

The nurse in the emergency room at the hospital registered surprise when she saw CJ. "I didn't expect to see you again so soon," she said.

"We need a gurney," CJ told her. "We have someone injured outside in a truck."

"Right away!" she said, and called for an orderly.

The emergency room doctor was with George for what seemed like hours. At last the nurse came into the waiting room. "Slight concussion," she said. "We'd like to keep her overnight for observation. She's right down the hall, third door to your left. The doctor's with her."

Nancy moved quickly down the hall and quietly opened the door to George's room. A young woman in a white jacket was standing by the bed.

"How is she, doctor?" Nancy whispered.

"I'm fine, Nan," George murmured, as she squinted at Nancy through half-opened eyes.

The doctor smiled. "Fine might be an overstatement," she said as Nancy introduced herself. "But she should be feeling better by morning." She motioned Nancy toward the door. "Right now she needs to rest. I think the worst thing she'll experience is a very bad headache."

Ned and CJ were waiting for her at the desk.

"Let's go over to the police station and get that over with," Nancy said wearily.

The officers who had picked up Kirby were waiting for them in a small conference room. Sergeant Whitcomb, the older man, pulled out a chair for Nancy and motioned for her to sit down across from him. "We've been in touch with the Emersonville police," he said. "And we've picked up Jennifer Bover." He shook his head in disbelief. "She sure doesn't look like someone who'd be mixed up with that pair," he said.

"What's going to happen to her?" Nancy asked.

Sergeant Whitcomb shook his head. "I don't know. Lieutenant Easterling's with her right now. I guess he hopped in his car not long after you talked to his sergeant," he said. "I don't have any problem booking Kirby. Not counting tonight's charges of kidnapping and assault with a deadly weapon, we've got enough on him now to lock him up for years. But I don't know about the girl. She probably saved your life. Easterling may cut a deal with her, if she agrees to testify against Kirby and the man they're holding in Emersonville."

There was a confusion of voices outside the room, and Sergeant Whitcomb got up and went to the door. "Down here!" he said, waving at someone. He turned to Nancy. "Do you mind if Easterling sits in while we talk?" he asked her. "You boys go and get yourselves some coffee," he said to Ned and CJ, without waiting for Nancy to answer. "There's a fresh pot in the front office."

"I don't mind," Nancy said. "It will save me from having to tell the whole story again."

"Just what I thought," said Sergeant Whitcomb.

When Nancy finished making her statement, Lieutenant Easterling leaned back in his chair and put his arms behind his head. "Sounds to me like you don't think Jennifer Bover's a criminal," he said, shrewdly eyeing Nancy.

"That's right. I don't," said Nancy. "I think she made a bad choice and got caught up in something that kept getting worse. I think she must be feeling very alone and scared."

Easterling nodded. "Right on both counts."

"May I talk to her?"

"Follow me." He stood up and led Nancy down the hall to a small room.

Jennifer was standing at the window, looking out on the street, when the door opened. She turned around at the sound, and Nancy could tell she'd been crying. Lieutenant Easterling sat down at a round table in the corner and shuffled some papers.

"Jennifer," Nancy said, walking toward her.

Jennifer looked at her hesitantly.

"Can we talk?" Nancy asked.

Jennifer nodded, and Nancy motioned her to one of the straight-backed chairs at the table.

But apparently the sight of Nancy was too much for Jennifer. Tears rolled down her cheeks, and sobs came from her throat in short bursts. "Why are you here?"

"Two reasons," Nancy replied. "First, I want

to thank you for following the van and telling the police which road we took."

Jennifer sniffed and nodded.

"You probably saved our lives," Nancy said. "And second, I want to help you."

"Why?" Jennifer asked. She blew her nose. "I'm so ashamed. I gave you nothing but grief! And if George hadn't been mistaken for me—" She stopped, and an anxious look crossed her face. "George!" she said. "Where is she?"

"She's in the hospital. Kirby cracked her on the head with his gun. Concussion, but she'll be okay. They'll release her tomorrow."

Just then Lieutenant Easterling cleared his throat. "This is unofficial," he said. "I'll take an official statement when we get back to Emersonville, but I'd like you to tell Nancy and me how you got mixed up in all this."

Jennifer nodded. "It seemed so innocent," she said. "Palumbo came into work one night with a package, all wrapped up, and said he had to get it to his friend, who was leaving for New York that night. Since I got off work at ten and he didn't get off until two, he asked me to deliver it. He said that there were documents in the package that his friend needed for a meeting in New York."

"Did he offer you money?"

"Not exactly. He said his friend would make it worth my while, that there was a lot of money at stake in the meeting and the documents were crucial to its success."

"So you agreed?"

"Sure. I didn't see anything wrong with dropping off a package." She got up and walked to the window. "The weird part came when he asked me to leave it on the steps of an apartment building on Montague Street. I mean, I figured if the documents were that important, I should hand them to somebody and not just leave them, but Palumbo said no. He said his friend would be watching for me and that it was too late at night to ring the bell. That I might disturb other people in the building or waken somebody's dog or something."

Nancy propped her elbows on the table and rested her chin in her hands. "Didn't you think that was odd?"

"Of course I did. I should have figured out right then that his friend didn't live in the building, but it was a one-time favor for a co-worker. I wasn't going to make a federal case out of it. I didn't know it would happen again."

"Did you deliver to the same place every time?" Lieutenant Easterling asked her.

Jennifer shook her head. "No, I made three deliveries to three different places. The second time he asked me to deliver a package, I was told to leave it on top of a garbage can in an alley. So I was definitely suspicious. I mean, this is a weird way to get something to a friend, right?"

"So why didn't you refuse?" Nancy asked.

Jennifer wiped her eyes with a tissue and took

a deep breath before answering. "Because he gave me two hundred dollars for delivering the first package," she said. She blew her nose. "I couldn't afford to turn it down. At least, that's what I thought then."

"Did you open the second package?" the lieutenant asked.

"No. But when he asked me the third time, I decided I had a right to know what I was delivering. So I opened that one."

"And found the emeralds," Nancy said.

Jennifer nodded. "They were the most beautiful things I'd ever seen. I tried them on. I loved them! I packaged the rest of the stuff back up and delivered it." Her voice grew soft. "But I kept the emeralds."

"Did you know they were stolen?"

"I suspected it, but I didn't know for sure until it was in the paper Thursday morning. The article said that there had been a burglary that hadn't been discovered until Wednesday, and the article mentioned the emeralds. I didn't know what to do then. All of a sudden I was part of a burglary ring. And to make matters worse, I was pretty certain that I'd been seen when I made that third drop."

Lieutenant Easterling shifted in the chair. "Where did you leave that package, Jennifer?" he asked.

"On a bench in the city park," she replied. "I thought I heard someone in the bushes, and I had a premonition—a spooky feeling—that I was being watched. I dropped the package and ran."

"Could you identify Kirby as the person who was watching you?" Nancy asked.

"No," Jennifer replied. "I never saw more than his shape in the shadows. But I knew he'd seen me. Suddenly I realized that he'd know there should have been emeralds in the package, once he opened it. I panicked. So I signed up for the bike trip—anything to get out of town—and I called in sick."

"And made an appointment to have your hair colored," Nancy added.

"Yes." Jennifer's voice was very small. "When things started going wrong on the trip, I suspected I'd been followed. But George looked more like me than I did, at that point."

"Why were you looking for a post office?" Nancy asked.

"I thought I'd mail the emeralds anonymously to the Emersonville police."

"And the bus?"

"I wanted to get away. Escape! I felt trapped."

"But you didn't ransack my room at Bannon or tamper with George's bike?" Nancy asked.

"No, no. That all must have been Michael— who thought George was me." She turned to Lieutenant Easterling. "What's going to happen now?"

His heavy gray brows furrowed over his blue

eyes. "Well," he said, "while your part in this can't be overlooked, you did assist in the apprehension of a criminal and probably saved the lives of two people. Also, you don't have a record. The judge may be lenient."

"Am I under arrest?"

"Not exactly," Lieutenant Easterling said. "I'm going to take you back to Emersonville tonight so you can talk to your attorney."

Jennifer looked up in surprise. "I don't have an attorney," she said.

Nancy smiled at her. "Yes, you do," she said. "I'll call my father. I'm sure he'll represent you."

Jennifer's eyes filled with tears. "How can I ever repay you?" she asked.

"No need," said Nancy. "See you at Emerson. Ned and CJ are waiting for me in the front office." She waved a quick goodbye and left.

The next morning the hospital called to say that George was being released. Nancy borrowed Mr. Kipling's truck for the short drive to Moorestown.

"Are you sure you're ready to get on that bike again?" she asked George as they drove back to pick up their things.

"Of course I'm ready! You don't think I'd let Erik beat me by default, do you?"

Nancy rolled her eyes upward in resignation. "George, you could have been killed last night.

There are half a dozen people who'd be glad to drive over here from Emerson and pick you up. You took such a whack on the head, I was sure you'd have a serious concussion or a fractured skull."

"Just another example of Kirby's stupidity," George said, peeling an orange she'd saved from her breakfast tray.

"What do you mean?" Nancy asked.

"If he'd been smart, he would have known how hardheaded I am!"

Nancy groaned.

"What's the story on Jennifer?"

Nancy shrugged. "I talked to Dad, and he thinks she'll get a suspended sentence. She'll probably have to do community service for a specified length of time."

Nancy pulled the truck up in front of the big house and took the keys in to Mr. Kipling, while George went to the cabin to get her things.

"Where's Kendra?" George asked CJ as she safety-checked her bike.

"She called her father to come and get her," he said. "She apologized to me about doctoring the water bottle before she left. She was pretty upset and embarrassed for listening to Kirby."

"She should be," George said indignantly. Then her voice softened. "Maybe she's learned something."

"Let's get moving!" Erik yelled.

CJ put his arm around George as they walked

their bikes to where the others were waiting. "How about dinner tonight?" he asked.

"You're on!" George said.

The sun was going down on a perfect autumn day when the cyclists rolled into Emerson. They locked their bikes and carried their gear into Packard Hall.

"Good news," Erik announced as he and George studied the time sheets.

Nancy leaned over and whispered to Ned. "If it's good for him, it's bad for George."

"I win!" Erik continued, turning to George. "By seven minutes and thirty-six seconds."

George flashed him a dirty look. "I do a whole lot better when nobody's trying to kill me."

Nancy grabbed her arm. "Come on, George. Ned and CJ are taking us out to dinner."

"At Ed's Diner?" George asked.

"Anywhere but," Nancy said with a grin. She hooked her arm into Ned's. "This is going to be a long, leisurely meal so Mr. Nickerson and I will have time to plan our *next* restful, uneventful three-day getaway!"

Nancy's next case:

Jack Broughton worked at Carson Drew's law firm. He also had a second, secret source of income: blackmail. But his scheme is dead, and so is he. Nancy found the body—now she's looking for the killer.

Broughton had a list of "clients" and a list of enemies to match. The question is, which one actually carried out the sentence of death? Never before has Nancy been so desperate to find an answer. Rumors are running wild in River Heights, and word is out that a top suspect in the case is none other than her own father, Carson Drew . . . in *FALSE PRETENSES*, Case #88 in The Nancy Drew Files™.